IT WAS QUIET . . . TOO QUIET . . .

There was something that set his nerves to jangling and didn't let him relax until he'd figured out what the problem was for certain. That jangling had only gotten louder in the back of Clint's mind when he'd stepped into the sitting room. In fact, as he looked around and slowly took in every unfamiliar corner and each dark shadow, Clint felt his grip close around the Colt's handle.

Clint was starting to wonder if he wasn't just being overly cautious when his eyes landed on what had been causing all of his tension. There was just a little glint of light streaming in from the hallway from under the door. There was some trickling in around the edges as well, and as he'd been watching, the light around the edge of the door got brighter.

The door wasn't closed all the way. Judging by the two shadows showing beneath the door, there was someone standing in the hall at that moment, pushing the door open . . .

THE GUNSMITH

260

FACES OF THE DEAD

J. R. ROBERTS

JOVE BOOKS, NEW YORK

FACES OF THE DEAD

A Jove Book / published by arrangement with
the author

PRINTING HISTORY
Jove edition / August 2003

ISBN: 0-515-13586-0

A JOVE BOOK®
Jove Books are published by The Berkley Publishing Group,
a division of Penguin Group (USA) Inc.,
375 Hudson Street, New York, New York 10014.
JOVE and the "J" design
are trademarks belonging to Penguin Group (USA) Inc.

PRINTED IN THE UNITED STATES OF AMERICA

10 9 8 7 6 5 4 3 2 1

ONE

Unlike most men, Clint Adams didn't get too big a portion of quiet moments and he'd learned a long time ago to savor each and every one of them. It had been a while since he'd ridden through Utah. In the last few towns he'd passed through, Clint noticed the younger crowd squawking about there being too much quiet for their tastes and not enough excitement.

In his younger days, Clint might have agreed with them. But like every other man who'd seen his share of birthdays, Clint was now more inclined to sit back and let the wind blow around him rather than fight to create a tornado. If a man waited long enough, a tornado would form just fine on its own.

Clint shook his head and felt the bite of irony in the back of his mind. He'd been just about to cut those thoughts short since such notions were only too likely to bring about bad news. A whole mess of superstitions came rattling through his mind. Most of them were just old sayings.

Let sleeping dogs lie.

Be careful what you wish for, because you just might get it.

And then there was an ancient curse he'd heard from

a Chinaman that went something like, *May you have an interesting life.*

Clint had to smile at those sayings because they were nothing more than superstitions themselves. The fact that he thought about them made him realize he wasn't any better than the gamblers afraid of jinxing themselves by wearing the wrong pair of socks or not touching their pocket watch enough times on the day of a high-stakes game.

When it all came down to it, Clint had to admit he believed in superstitions or whatever he wanted to call them to some extent or another. Besides, he sure as hell didn't have any good explanation for half the wild things he'd seen in his lifetime. Bad luck was just as good a way to describe it as any other.

Pulling up the collar of his jacket, Clint braced himself against a particularly chilling wind that whipped through the trees and seemed to tear through his entire body. Eclipse shuddered as well at the touch of autumn's bare hand and the muscles twitched beneath the Darley Arabian's sleek coat.

The cold gust seemed to shake Clint out of his musings and snap him back into the real world. He was the last one who could complain about bad luck. With all the men taking shots at him, the fact that he was still alive at all should have been a testament to all kinds of good luck.

Or maybe just dumb luck.

Clint grinned to himself and wrapped Eclipse's reins around his fist before tapping the stallion's sides with his heels. A good run would do them both some good and get the blood flowing through their veins. It would be another few day's ride before he reached the next town, according to the directions of one of those babbling old men who never seemed to stop trying to predict the weather.

Letting out a huffing breath, Eclipse broke into a gallop

and then a full run. Clint was once again reminded of tornadoes as Eclipse whipped over the path, kicking up dead leaves and pebbles in his wake. Behind them, there was a trail of dust and debris hanging in the air like a smudge upon a canvas marking where they'd just been.

Before the stallion could get too tired, Clint reined him in and slowed Eclipse to a walk. His ears were ringing with the thunder of the stallion's hooves and Clint allowed himself some time to let the noise fade away. When it didn't, he concentrated on what he'd thought were just stubborn echoes.

The pounding of hooves could still be heard. In fact, the more he thought about it, the louder it got. He gave it a few more seconds; once he concentrated a bit, he could tell two facts right away.

First of all, the noise he heard was no echo. There was another horse galloping not too far away.

Second, that horse was getting closer by the second.

Clint turned around in his saddle and took a look over his shoulder. The trail he'd been on for the last several days was bordered on both sides by a fair amount of trees, but not so many that riding between them would have been impossible. The sounds he'd heard, however, were coming too quickly for the animal making them to be doing anything but running flat out. Also, he couldn't hear any signs of snapping branches or a single impact of a racing body scraping against a tree trunk.

Clint only had to wait a couple more seconds before he could see what was making all the noise. It was a horse, that much was obvious. But when he got a look at it, Clint could also see there was someone riding on the horse who didn't seem too concerned about stopping it.

Out of common courtesy, Clint steered Eclipse to a wide spot along the side of the trail so the rider could get on by. He kept his eyes on that animal, however, since it seemed to be more wild than anything else.

As it ran, the horse veered from side to side, snorting loudly and charging with every bit of strength it had. For a second, it seemed to be heading straight for Clint and Eclipse. Then, at the last possible second, it veered off and thundered past, leaving less than an inch between itself and a painful collision with the Darley Arabian waiting just off the trail.

Clint wasn't too concerned about the near-miss with the stampeding animal. He was more concerned with the state of its rider. As far as he could tell, the figure atop the horse was about to fall out of the saddle completely. In fact, judging by the passing glimpse he'd gotten, Clint figured the man might have been passed out already.

"Damn," Clint said as he snapped Eclipse's reins. "Talk about your bad luck."

TWO

Even after the run he'd just had, Eclipse was more than willing to take off after the horse that had just stormed past him. The Darley Arabian let out an anxious whinny before surging forward with every ounce of strength his legs could muster.

Clint held on tightly and hunkered down, knowing full well what the stallion was capable of. The trail took a sharp left turn not too far ahead of where they'd started, which put the first horse temporarily out of Clint's field of vision. Leaning into the turn as Eclipse tore into it, Clint quickly got the first horse back in his sights and snapped the reins.

Now that he'd matched the first horse's speed, Clint could get a better look at both that animal and its rider. The figure in the saddle was most definitely a man, since it had wide shoulders and a thick torso. The arms and legs were too thick to belong to a woman. More than that, Clint simply couldn't think of a woman who could hold onto a horse going that fast and moving that wildly. Come to think of it, Clint was beginning to wonder how anyone besides a rodeo star could hang on to an animal moving like that.

The man riding ahead of him wasn't keeping low or even trying to move with the animal beneath him. Instead, he just sat up straight and bounced like a buoy in a hurricane. That was what had gotten Clint worried that the rider might be unconscious.

The longer Clint watched, however, the more he thought the rider couldn't possibly be unconscious. Otherwise, he would have surely been thrown from the horse's back altogether. Rather than hang back and debate the how's and why's like an old man pondering the weather, Clint focused on catching up to that horse before it either broke its legs, threw its rider, or charged through some unsuspecting campsite like a miniature stampede.

Clint pressed his heels into Eclipse's sides just enough to let the stallion know he meant business. The Darley Arabian responded instantly to the request and poured on the remainder of its reserve strength. Each breath started blasting through the horse's nostrils like steam, and its head pumped forward like a piston.

The distance between Eclipse and the wild horse closed rapidly. In a matter of seconds, Clint was able to start reaching out with one hand to get a feel for the second horse. One touch was all he needed to feel the sticky sweat on the animal's coat. Its muscular body was hot and had obviously been pushed to its limits for quite a while. But even more than feeling as though it was straining itself, the horse seemed panicked and scared. Clint could get that much off of the animal just by being close to it for more than a second or two.

Suddenly, as though it was reacting to the presence of another living creature that had gotten too close to it, the frightened horse lifted its head and let out a bellowing whinny. The creature started to buck, but instead of rearing up all the way and throwing the rider off its back, it twisted away from Eclipse and leaped off the beaten path.

Clint hadn't been able to get a good look at the rider before the horse quickly changed direction. The other animal had been in such a hurry that its flank bumped into

Eclipse and nearly threw the Darley Arabian off its footing.

If he hadn't been going at top speed, Eclipse wouldn't have been affected at all by the mild collision. But since he was straining himself close to his own limit, the stallion shuddered slightly when he felt the other horse bump into his flank.

It wasn't much, but that little jostle was nearly enough to twist Eclipse's hoof the wrong way, which might have turned out very badly for himself and Clint as well. The trail was uneven enough at normal speeds, but with the trees whipping by and the rocks sailing underfoot, every misstep was a possible disaster.

Clint reacted instinctively and got Eclipse back under control. Having been raised in the circus, Eclipse took well to the direction and didn't seem to panic in the slightest. All the same, Clint could feel that he'd been within a hair's width of eating a portion of the trail for dinner.

By the time he'd righted himself in the saddle and started looking around for the other horse again, Clint realized that the panicked animal was nowhere to be seen. He let his ears guide him since the sound of the other horse's frantic running could still be heard over the pounding of Eclipse's hooves.

Turning his upper body and pulling on the reins at the same time, Clint brought Eclipse around like an extension of his own torso as he shifted to chase down the other animal. By this time, Clint was more than convinced that the rider was in serious trouble. Even if the man could hang on no matter what the horse did, that frightened animal was on the way to hurting itself as well and Clint didn't want to see that happen either.

Facing the edge of the trail, Clint was just in time to see the frightened horse leap through a break in the surrounding trees. He guided Eclipse by shifting his position on the saddle as well as steering with the reins. Having grown accustomed to one another through years of partnership, the pair moved like a single body, one quickly adjusting to accommodate the other.

Eclipse turned hard to the left, landed on both front hooves, and twisted to the right. From there, he planted his back hooves and pushed off into a jump that launched them through the opening that the first horse had just broken through like a brick through a window. Covering more distance than height, the jump ended on the other side of the trees where Eclipse started to gallop after the wild and panicked animal.

Although he was impressed by the maneuver, Clint couldn't take too long to admire it since his brain was already going through a fevered set of its own calculations. With the trees spaced unevenly and the ground becoming more and more unsteady as they broke farther away from the trail, he had to figure the perfect angle to approach the other horse. Besides that, he had to worry about spooking the beast any more than it already was.

But there was something even more pressing in Clint's thoughts. As he tried to draw up to the crazed animal while preparing to dodge the rider who looked about ready to fall off at any moment, he pictured where they were in relation to the terrain marked on his map. He wasn't intimately familiar with the state, but he knew enough about its terrain.

More importantly, he knew there was a gorge somewhere nearby. The instant he got their position squared away in his mind, the trees opened up in front of them and the ground fell away into cold, empty space.

THREE

"Jesus Christ!" Clint shouted when he saw that the supply of ground directly in front of him was running out fast. The words came out of him in a reflexive grunt and were immediately swallowed up by the air, which rushed past his head in a speeding torrent.

His eyes took everything in that they could, much the same way they did when he found himself staring down the wrong end of a gun. The world seemed to shift into a slower pace and he instinctively looked around in every direction for something that might be used to save his skin.

The first thing he noticed was that the edge of the gorge wasn't so close that it couldn't be avoided. On the other hand, seeing as he only had about twenty feet or so and was riding toward it at full speed, he was going to have to act damn quick to keep from charging over the side.

The next thing he noticed was that the horse directly in front of him didn't seem to have any qualms about running in a straight line. It was too frightened to notice anything but the open air at the end of its nose.

Clint wasn't worried about getting Eclipse to turn away from the edge with plenty of time to spare. On the other hand, he wasn't too anxious to watch a living creature plummet to its death with a man on its back who didn't seem worried about going for the last ride of his life.

The figure in the wild horse's saddle shifted every so often, but only when the horse made an exaggerated movement. Clint couldn't tell if the rider was unconscious or just out of his mind, but he wasn't about to waste his time going over the details. Instead, he took his eyes away from the rider and focused once again on the horse and the dwindling amount of trail leading up to one hell of a drop.

Clint wrapped the reins tightly around his left fist and steered Eclipse over to the other horse's left side. From there, he dug his heels into the Darley Arabian's sides to coax that last bit of speed out of the horse's reserves. It wasn't the way he preferred to treat Eclipse, but it was enough to get the stallion up alongside the other horse in less than two seconds flat.

Having already gotten that close to the horse not too long ago, Clint knew that the animal was too panicked to be calmed in the short amount of time that was left. Rather than try to take the reins from where he was sitting, he stood up in his stirrups and set his left foot on the saddle.

There wasn't enough time for Clint to think about the sanity of what he was about to do. Luckily, there also wasn't enough time for him to get thrown too far off balance by the irregular jostling of Eclipse's strides. Just as the Darley Arabian shifted to make up for a dent in the ground, Clint pushed up and away with both feet, launching himself toward the wild horse while simultaneously pushing Eclipse away from the edge of the gorge.

By his quick mental calculations, Clint figured he was about to run out of solid ground at any moment. It seemed as though he was flying through the air for an eternity and just as he was starting to think that he was falling over the side, he landed roughly upon the horse's back. His legs dropped down on either side of the animal, placing him just between the saddle horn and the horse's neck. Although he started to slide off, Clint managed to right himself before it was too late.

He knew he was already out of time and that he might have just done one of the craziest stunts he'd ever dreamed up. As he thought those things, Clint reached out with both hands to grab hold of the reins right where they connected to the bit in the horse's mouth. As soon as his fingers closed around leather, he pulled back and to the left with every bit of strength he had.

The horse responded, more out of instinct than anything else. Its muscles were still working like a runaway train and its eyes were still frightened and glazed over, but it obeyed the harsh command as Clint twisted its head to one side.

Veering to the left, the horse let out a scared whinny that squeezed its ribs together like massive bellows. Clint could feel the animal pawing at the ground and knew that the horse was skidding upon loose dirt and gravel. At that moment, he felt the horse's back end drop down like a wagon that had suddenly lost a wheel.

He lowered himself over the animal's neck and grabbed on tightly, knowing that one of its legs had just slipped over the edge of the gorge. "Hang on!" Clint hollered to the man behind him, unsure whether the rider could hear him or not. But those words were for himself as much as anyone else and he did his best to heed them.

Clint could tell the weight of his body was putting a hell of a lot of strain on the horse's front legs. Not only was he aware of that, but he was counting on it since he was also praying that his weight would be enough to anchor the animal rather than let them both slide over the side.

As the horse kept skidding and pawing at the ground, Clint prepared himself for the moment when he might have to jump off and save his own hide. He put that off as long as he could until he felt the horse's body shift once again beneath him.

The back end of the animal jolted and bucked, causing the bottom to drop out of Clint's stomach. But rather than slide toward the deadly drop, the horse was pushing itself forward. Clint's weight had not only allowed it to hang on, but had also forced it to slow down and finally stop.

As soon as he could tell that they were on solid ground and no longer stampeding recklessly through the trees, Clint loosened his grip on the horse's neck and swung down off of the beast entirely. Even after all that had happened, he still felt bad when he heard the pained groan that came from the horse's straining breaths.

Clint could feel his own heart slamming inside his chest, but pushed that aside as he regained his balance and turned to reach out for the sweating, wheezing animal next to him. "Easy now," he said to the horse while stroking the side of its head. "Take a breath and slow it down." Knowing that the horse couldn't understand his words, Clint kept talking in a soothing tone, which at least took some of the panic from the animal's eyes.

"That's better," Clint said once he was sure the horse wasn't about to bolt. Turning to look up at the rider, Clint wiped the sweat from his own brow and said, "Now what about you? How'd you manage to hang on through so much—"

But Clint didn't bother finishing his question.

There was no need.

A dead man wouldn't answer him anyway.

FOUR

Having burned off all the steam it had built up, the horse that had found Clint all but collapsed under its own weight. Every step it took as Clint led it deeper into the trees was painful for the animal and it was more than happy to stop once its reins were tied around a thin trunk.

Clint watched as Eclipse walked up to him and nuzzled his shoulder with his nose. The Darley Arabian seemed just as glad to see Clint as Clint was glad to feel solid ground beneath his boots.

After a few quick pats on the snout, Clint tied Eclipse next to the other horse and then turned his attention to the man in that animal's saddle. Now that they weren't running at full speed, it was much easier to see why that man hadn't done much to save himself or his horse when they'd been rampaging through the trees.

The other rider's skin was pale and waxy, hanging off his bones like a hide that had been draped over the back of a chair. His features drooped on him as if they'd been poorly drawn onto the front of his skull. There were scars scattered over his cheeks and forehead, but very little blood. By the looks of his filthy skin, the dead man might have been dragged facedown through a mud hole. When he looked a little closer, Clint saw that it wasn't dirt smeared into his skin. Instead, it was the blood that he'd overlooked the first time he'd checked the body over.

The dead man's blood was a dark, crusted layer that nearly covered every square inch of the man's head and neck. Clint never got used to sights as ugly as this one. That sight in particular was surely going to haunt his memories for a good, long time.

Clint looked away from the corpse's face and noticed that the body was tied onto the saddle by thick coils of rope wrapped around his legs and body. There was so much rope, in fact, that Clint had first thought the man in the saddle was physically bigger than he truly was. It just so happened that the rope added bulk to the figure like so much straw stuffed into an empty set of clothes.

He didn't really want to deal with the body at that particular moment, but Clint reached for the knife in his boot, which was always hidden there when he was on the road. That blade had seen him through some tough times, although mostly as an observer.

Clint drew the knife and started cutting his way through the length of stiff, dirty rope. If not for the exhausted wheezing coming from the dead man's horse, Clint might have just let the corpse sit where it was until he got some rest for himself. He figured once the work was done, everyone could rest soundly whether they stood on two legs or four.

Clint's knife ran over the outside of the rope as though the blade hadn't even been sharpened. Once he started leaning into it and pushing down with his back behind it, Clint felt the steel begin to cut through the strands. Finally, after slicing through the hardened outer layer, he got down to the rope's inner strands and then all the way through to the other side.

The muscles in his arms and shoulder were burning by the time he was able to free the corpse's legs. After trying to pull to body down, he realized there was another rope completely tying the torso to the saddle. Letting out a tired, frustrated breath, Clint got to work cutting through the second rope, cursing every word that had come out of his mouth doubting the existence of bad luck.

There was still a fair amount of light in the sky when Clint's task was finally done. Even so, he felt as though he'd been working well through the night. His arms were tired from hacking through the tough ropes and he still had to get the body down from on top of the horse. As if sensing that he wanted to take a break before finishing what he was doing, the other horse began to shudder and shift from one foot to another.

"All right," Clint said. "I won't leave all that on top of you. Just give me a moment to catch my breath."

Sucking in a lungful of the cool air, Clint steeled himself and reached up to take hold of the body by its arm. He tugged it once toward him and was relieved to notice that the corpse was no longer tied down by any more of the ropes that Clint had so quickly grown to hate. All it took was a second pull and Clint braced himself to catch the body as it slowly toppled from its perch.

As soon as the body fell off, the horse shook its head and let out a sound that was unmistakably grateful.

"Sure, you feel better." Clint grunted as he took the weight of the body into his arms and over his shoulder. "Too bad you can't help me out in return."

But Clint was on his own. Without stopping to let the dead weight settle completely onto him, he diverted the corpse's momentum until he could lower it to the ground and roll it onto its back. The sound of that body hitting the dirt was one of the best things Clint had heard all day. Hell, it was the best thing he'd heard all week. Once he heard that sound, Clint knew he could let himself take a seat on the ground and give himself a moment to catch his breath.

Then again, it was kind of hard for him to relax too much with a dead body lying within arm's reach.

Unable to put it off any longer, Clint turned toward the corpse and knelt down beside it. "All right," he muttered while starting to dig through the dead man's pockets. "Let's see what you can tell me."

FIVE

Clint wasn't exactly sure what he was going to find when he began poking around in the dead man's shirt pockets, but he did know for certain the man had died by lead poisoning. There was a bullet hole through the corpse's chest. Since it was obvious that the man hadn't tied himself to that horse, Clint figured his pockets would be empty as well. That didn't bother him simply because he wasn't in the business of making money from robbing corpses.

What Clint was hoping for was something that might let him know who the man was or what might have landed him on top of a wild horse headed over the side of a gorge. It wasn't every day that Clint was forced to risk his life in that particular manner, so he was rightfully curious as to how he'd wound up in that position.

Clint had seen his fair share of dead bodies. Such sights weren't his favorites, but whenever he stared at the face of a dead man, it was usually through a haze of gun smoke. As he patted his hands along the corpse's pockets, Clint stared down at the other man's face. No matter how much he wanted to look away, he simply couldn't get himself to do so.

In his brain, dozens of other faces were kicked up from his past. Some of them were images he hadn't thought of

17

in years and came as a surprise that he remembered them
at all. Some of them were friends and some were men
who'd wanted to kill him. The only thing they all had in
common were that they were faces of the dead.

Looking back upon them was never easy, especially
since Clint had been the one to put most of them into
their graves.

He found nothing in the shirt pockets or the pockets
of the man's jeans. Although Clint was getting used to
the uncomfortable task, he was still anxious to be done
with it. Having searched the worst pockets first, he then
moved his attention to the dead man's jacket.

It was a lot easier rifling through the jacket since he
didn't have to touch the corpse directly. The longer he
took in trying to look for clues upon the dead man, however, the more he was feeling like a ghoul for having even
started the grisly task.

Just as he was about to call an end to his morbid
search, Clint found something in one of the jacket's inside
pockets. He detected something in one of the outer pockets as well and rather than stay there next to the corpse,
Clint removed the jacket and stood up. He took the jacket
with him as he turned away from the body and put a few
steps between it and him.

He felt instantly better once he could see something
else besides that corpse and those dead eyes glaring back
up at him. The faces of all those other men from his past
began to fade. Finally, after a deep breath or two, they
were gone. But Clint didn't kid himself in the slightest.
Those faces might be gone, but he knew damn well they
weren't staying away.

Clint walked over to a tree not too far from where he'd
tied Eclipse. The Darley Arabian looked over to him and
locked eyes with Clint as though he was concerned about
his owner's well-being. All Clint had to do was nod once

and the stallion went back to grazing on what little patches of grass there were nearby.

The wheezing coming from the other horse had subsided a bit, having turned into something more like a steady current of air. Clint looked over to check on that animal and saw it was sleeping. Its large head hung down like a sack of mail dangling from a hook. Only that deep breathing told Clint the animal was alive at all.

Leaning back against the tree, Clint closed his eyes for a second and rolled his head back and forth to work out some of the kinks in his neck. Another face drifted into his memory just then, except this one belonged to a friend of his that was very much alive. Rick Hartman was the man's name and he owned a saloon called Rick's Place down in Labyrinth, Texas.

Clint smiled to himself because he knew if Rick was sitting there next to him, he would say, "Dammit, Clint. You're getting too damn old to be jumping around like that. And messin' with a dead man, to boot! You're too damn old for that kind of nonsense, too."

Rick had been there at the beginning of a lot of interesting times in Clint's life. And by "interesting," Clint figured he meant dangerous. Lots of trouble had found Clint when he was having a beer at Rick's Place. But then again, trouble seemed to find Clint no matter where he hung his hat. And Clint was starting to get the sneaking suspicion that he was about to find a bit more trouble once he set his eyes upon whatever was inside the dead man's pockets.

Even as he imagined Rick Hartman shaking his head and rolling his eyes, Clint picked up that dusty jacket and slipped his hand inside the first pocket.

SIX

The first pocket Clint checked was on the right-hand side and was an outer pocket covered by a battered leather flap. There was a buttonhole in the flap, but only a bit of frayed string where the button itself should have been. Inside that pocket, Clint felt a hunk of metal and a length of thin chain. He already had an idea of what was inside there even before he pulled his hand out to take a look.

Sure enough, his first guess would have been correct. It was a pocket watch. The timepiece wasn't much to look at, at least not on the outside. Its cover was tarnished brass and scarred with several dents and chips that would be picked up after years of being carried around. The chain was tipped with a fob used for connecting to a hole in a man's vest or possibly a shirt. The fob was dented as well as stained a shade of light brown and when Clint lifted it to his nose, he distinctly recognized the odor of tobacco.

Clint pressed down on the little button on top of the watch, which caused the dented cover to flip open. Inside, the watch looked like something altogether different than what Clint had been holding in his hand only a fraction of a second ago. The watch's face was so well-maintained that he had to tap the glass covering the hands to make sure the protective layer was even still intact. Ornate gold hands were poised over a pearl face where black Roman numerals were impressively engraved.

When Clint twisted the knob on top of the watch a few times, the secondhand started making its rounds over the numerals as a tune began to play from within the watch itself. He couldn't recognize the tune as the high-pitched notes tinkled from within the watch, but Clint had to admit it was a pretty song.

Rather than listen to the music, Clint shut the watch and turned it over. Once again, his instincts were correct and there was an engraving on the back of the timepiece. It read *Partners* in simple, elegant lettering.

That watch alone told Clint a whole lot. The first thing that jumped into his mind was that, since a watch like that was still in the dead man's pocket at all, it was certain whoever had tied him to that horse wasn't just a robber. It also told him that someone the dead man had known liked him enough to give him such an extravagant gift. Judging by the brass exterior, the watch had been in that man's pocket for a number of years.

There were still plenty of questions running through Clint's mind. Rather than focus on those, however, he set the watch down and looked into the second outer pocket, which appeared to have something stuffed inside of it.

Clint pulled out a small bundle of folded papers, which were tied together by a piece of twine. The papers were stiff and not folded completely in half, since they were actually a stack of photographs.

Once the twine was removed, Clint unfolded the pictures and took a look at the one on top. Roughly the size of a preacher's Bible, the picture was of three people standing with their arms around each other's shoulders in front of what appeared to be a house or even possibly a store. Two of the people in the black and white image were women. One had either brown or red hair and the other was unmistakably blonde.

The blonde was wearing the remnants of a smile, even after standing in the same spot for enough time that was usually enough to put a frown on most people's faces when getting their picture taken. Her hair flowed down over her shoulders and had obviously been specially primped for that picture. She was dressed in a light-colored dress and held onto the person next to her with casual affection. Her other hand was reaching up to the back of her head, putting her in a pose similar to that of a stage actress.

On the opposite side of the picture, the second woman appeared to be just as happy as the blonde. Her smile was a little more subdued but it was there all the same. Dark hair was swept over to one side, where it was gathered up by a ribbon and set over her right shoulder. As much as Clint stared at the picture, he couldn't be completely certain as to the color of the woman's hair. He decided it was probably red, since her skin was the lighter shade more common in redheads.

Unlike the blonde, the redhead seemed to be staring right through the camera's lens and into the eyes of whomever might be admiring her image. Even in the photo, her eyes reflected confidence and determination. They were strong, piercing eyes that held Clint's gaze almost as strongly as she was holding on to the man beside her.

Having studied both women, since they were the ones who naturally caught his eye first, Clint looked at the figure standing in between them. He had to hold the sides of the picture apart a bit more to get a good look, and found himself glancing over to the corpse that had previously owned the photo. The one in the middle of the picture, his face and body split down the middle by a crease in the photo, was the man who now lay dead a few yards away from Clint's feet.

At first, the face in the center of that picture just struck

Clint as vaguely familiar. It took a few looks back and forth for comparison, but finally Clint was able to see through the layers of blood and grime that stained the corpse's face. Once he could see past the dirt and death, it wasn't too much of a jump to see that the body's face and the one smiling in the picture between those two women were both one and the same.

Needless to say, the man looked a whole lot happier in the picture than he did at the moment. Not only was he in between two beautiful women, but he was alive and well. Clint would have paid good money to know what the man was thinking when that picture had been taken. Whatever it was, it hadn't been enough to even put a dent in the grin that was plastered on his face.

Smiles that wide were rare sights in any photograph. In fact, most folks wound up looking more like corpses after the camera finally completed the task of copying their image. But the man in that picture looked like he'd just been told a joke after raking in a heaping stack of chips at the end of the best day of his life. Not only did he look happy, but he looked about to bust.

In a strange way, Clint couldn't help but be a little jealous. After all, that man was obviously having the time of his life with two very attractive women. He could only imagine what had gone on before to put the smile on that man's face. That particular sentiment lasted a whole second until he took another look at where that smiling man was now.

SEVEN

The rest of the pictures were of the dead man and those same two women. One was just of him and the blonde and the other was just him and the redhead. The last picture was of the two women together and that was the only one where neither of the subjects were smiling.

Clint found that last photo the most interesting of the lot. It wasn't the best to look at and didn't even make either of the women look especially attractive. It did give him the impression that although the dead man liked being with them and they liked being with him, those two women didn't seem to like being around each other. They didn't like it one bit.

Once he was done with the pictures, Clint folded them back in half and retied the twine around the middle of the bundle. He set them down next to the watch and went back to rummaging through the jacket pockets. There was a small pocket on the outside over the chest, but there was nothing in that besides a crushed match.

Laying the jacket open on the ground, Clint then felt inside the inner right pocket. There was some folded papers that felt like newsprint or possibly pages torn from a book. When he tried to feel what was at the bottom of the pocket, Clint's hand emerged through a rip where the pocket had been sewn into the lining.

All but a quarter of an inch or so was torn from the bottom seam, but that had apparently been enough to keep the paper from falling out. Clint removed the paper from the pocket and saw that it was actually a letter folded and sealed with a bit of gritty, melted wax.

If the dead man had been meaning to mail the letter, he didn't have enough money to pay for a proper envelope. Instead, the letter had been folded twice and sealed. The address, written on the back of the paper in a hasty scrawl which Clint could barely read, was made out to Bonnie Shaughnessey in Estes Canyon, Utah.

Upon reading that name, Clint immediately pictured the redhead in the photograph he'd found. He even took another look at the picture to see if the name seemed to fit her or the blonde. Of course there was no way for him to tell, until he finally got an idea that made him feel more than a little stupid. It wasn't a bad idea, but he felt stupid for not having thought to do it before.

The picture on top of the stack was of the dead man with both of the women. Clint turned the picture over and, sure enough, there was writing on the back in that same, hasty scrawl. Rick would have gotten a good laugh out of the fact that Clint hadn't thought to look on the back of the pictures before.

"Nice detective work," Hartman said in Clint's head. "Better stick to that gun of yours if you want to make a decent living."

Clint laughed to himself and turned the whole stack of pictures over to read what was written on the other side.

The first one had, "Me and the girls" written on the back.

The next one said, "Me and Luanne."

Written on the back of the third was, "Me and Bonnie."

Clint turned that picture over again and grinned triumphantly when he found himself looking at the dead man standing next to the redhead. So that was Bonnie.

He didn't need to flex too many mental muscles to figure out the blonde's name was Luanne. Just to cap things off, he flipped to the last picture in the group and read what was written.

"Bonnie and Luanne."

Big surprise.

Out of curiosity, Clint went back to the letter and started to break the crude wax seal holding the paper folded together. He got far enough to see the lines of handwritten text before stopping. Clint froze in place, his eyes wandering up from the letter and his fingers still testing the strength of the seal.

Looking at the body laying there, Clint couldn't get himself to open that letter. He didn't feel bad about going through the dead man's pockets since he was only looking for pieces to a puzzle. That letter, on the other hand, was something specifically not meant for his eyes. The only person intended to read what was written there was Bonnie Shaughnessey of Estes Canyon, Utah.

After deliberating a couple seconds longer, Clint finally took the letter and set it on the ground with the watch on top of it so a stray wind wouldn't take it away. That only left one more pocket for him to check and Clint leaned toward the jacket so he could do that very thing.

The inner-left-hand pocket appeared to have more in it than any of the rest. In fact, Clint remembered that pocket as being the one to truly catch his attention when he was searching the body. Whatever was in that pocket was bulky enough to even stand out when the dead man was wearing the jacket, and Clint had been thinking about those bulky contents the entire time he'd looked through the rest.

Perhaps some part of him considered saving the best part for last. It seemed an almost silly notion considering what he was doing, but that silly notion had gotten him to hold off in reaching into that pocket, all the same.

Now that it was time to see what was inside that pocket, Clint felt the anticipation building up at the bottom of his stomach. He wasn't so much excited as anxious since he had no clue what could be in there. His hand slipped into the large inner pocket and came upon a fat bundle of cloth. It might have been a bandanna or rags, but whatever it was, the cloth was wadded up and stuffed into the pocket.

At first, Clint was disappointed. His mind was working on trying to figure who this man was or what had happened to him and the one clue he'd been saving turned out to be a wad of cloth. But when his hand closed around the cloth, he felt that anticipation build up once again inside of him.

There was something else in that pocket. It was something wrapped up inside the cloth.

Clint pulled back the layers of cloth until he was beginning to think he'd imagined the fact that anything else was inside. Finally, after pulling away one more strip of dirty material, he looked down at what had been bundled up so thoroughly.

It took him a moment to realize what he was seeing. Then, once he knew, he could hardly believe it.

Lying in the folds of cloth was a severed tongue.

EIGHT

With the bundle still in his hand, Clint walked over to the body and lowered himself to one knee beside it. He used his free hand to take hold of the man's chin and start pulling down.

The mouth looked more like a dark hole that had been dug into the dead man's face. The jaw was still and it took a good deal of work to finally get it open. The bones scraped loudly against each other as they moved apart, but after a bit of work, Clint was able to get a look inside.

Several of the dead man's teeth were chipped, cracked, or missing entirely. The ones that were there were covered with caked-on blood that was nearly indistinguishable from dirt. Clint could barely tell the difference in the fading light, but decided most of it was blood since the coppery stench of it practically reached out to smack him across the face.

Holding his breath, Clint opened the jaw a little more and tilted his head to get a better look toward the back of the gaping mouth. Besides the incomplete collection of teeth and crusted blood, all he could see was a ragged stump of shriveled flesh sticking up from the back of his throat.

That answered the most recent question in Clint's mind.

Not only was that a tongue he was holding, but it was the tongue that belonged in the mouth into which he was currently looking.

Having seen more than enough for one day, Clint pushed the dead man's mouth shut and covered up the tongue in his hand. Not only did he wrap the grisly piece of flesh in the rags where he'd found it, but he also added some more wrappings of his own. Clint wrapped a bandanna and a scarf that had been in his saddlebag until he couldn't even feel the shape of the tongue through all its wrappings.

From there, he stuffed the bundle back into the pocket where he'd found it and used the jacket to cover the dead man's face. With the sun disappearing over the horizon, the shape of the corpse on the ground started to look more like a log or a long stack of firewood.

Clint walked over to the dead man's horse and patted the animal's neck until he could feel the shaking stop. The horse was probably the one thing within ten miles that was more tired than Clint, himself. For that reason alone, Clint felt obliged to make sure the poor thing had a good night's sleep.

Eclipse didn't seem to mind giving up some of the feed that was kept in Clint's bags as a last resort in case they found themselves in a spot with no place to graze. Cupping his hand, Clint held up the mixture of oats to the horse's mouth, where they were sucked down in no time flat.

After retrieving his bedroll, Clint stretched out on the ground far away from the body and stared up at the sky. He let his eyes wander over the dark blue blanket over his head until it shifted to an oily black. The stars made their appearance one at a time until they were spread out in every direction like a spill of diamond dust over black velvet.

Although there was nothing to beat the comfort of a

mattress and pillow beneath him, the open country had special comforts of its own. Those stars were one, but so was the wind that moved over him and brushed across his face like a lover's hand.

It was quiet at night if a man got himself far enough away from civilization. Sure there were towns within a day's ride or so, but as long as they were out of sight the noise they made didn't get a chance to spoil what he heard at that moment.

Nothing.

Absolutely nothing.

After a few moments, the rustle of wind through the leaves faded away much like the ticking of a clock that was always next to someone's desk. Clint just didn't hear it anymore and that suited him fine. There were no voices yelling or doors slamming. There were no wagon wheels rolling by or any other irregular noises that couldn't fit so easily into the background.

Having that much quiet all around him made it that much easier for Clint to think. Once all the excitement had gone away and the blood wasn't pumping through his veins like so much rushing water, Clint took a look back upon what he'd found with a clear head.

Whoever the man was, he wasn't robbed.

The man was most definitely killed.

Clint also knew that the man had some connection to Bonnie Shaughnessey in Estes Canyon. Not only did he know where that was, but a little quick figuring was all it took for Clint to be fairly certain he could get there within two or three days. Two or three days in the company of a body that wasn't about to get any fresher.

Just to be on the safe side, Clint figured in a couple hours to dig the grave, which pushed the travel time to three days at the maximum. And once he was at Estes Canyon, he planned to do . . . what?

Find out who the dead man was?

Find out who'd killed him?

Maybe all of those things and maybe even more. The one thing he knew for sure was that Bonnie Shaughnessey was waiting for her letter. Clint wasn't normally in the mail delivery business, but this was a very special exception.

NINE

It took Clint several hours to find a suitable burial spot and dig a hole deep enough to keep the dead man from being picked out of the ground by scavengers. He started in on the task as soon as he woke up the next morning, wanting to get done with the job even before he took time for breakfast.

Once that was done, he tied up the man's belongings and strapped them onto the back of his horse. Now that it had had time to calm down and get some rest, the other horse turned out to be quite calm and even-tempered. It rode next to Eclipse the entire day without Clint having to do anything but tie the reins to the Darley Arabian's saddle horn. It was rare the animal even let much slack form in the leather straps.

Clint took it easy for the first day's ride, allowing mostly for the dead man's horse to fully recover from the strain of the past few days. The next day, however, was strictly to cover as much ground in as little time as possible. Clint rode at a good pace and both horses seemed more than up to the task. Eclipse was always ready for a run and the other horse kept up without too much problem. Along the way, Clint filled his time by thinking about everything he'd found in the dead man's pockets and how they could all piece together to form a clearer picture.

He was no detective, but there wasn't a whole lot to do when the only thing to fill his day was keeping on top of his horse. Thankfully, Estes Canyon wasn't as far as he'd been thinking and by sundown on that second day of riding he could see the first hints of civilization.

He'd been just about to start looking for a campsite when the sun was lost behind the horizon and a bank of clouds. In that light, it was easier to pick out the blocky shapes of buildings in the distance. Just before it dropped out of sight completely, the sun threw a few of its rays onto a row of windowpanes that winked at Clint like a beacon.

Shading his eyes and squinting into the last traces of dusk, Clint spotted the town. He snapped Eclipse's reins and headed straight for those buildings, his mouth already watering for a hot meal that consisted of more than two ingredients.

The path turned into a street in less than an hour and soon Clint was picking up the scent of steaks being cooked to perfection. It wasn't hard to find where that smell was coming from since one of the nearby buildings was marked by a sign that simply read PAPPY'S STEAK-HOUSE.

Clint didn't care about much of anything else at that point. Once he spotted the restaurant and saw enough space at a nearby hitching post for both horses, he was out of the saddle and tying both reins onto the wooden rail. He took one step up toward the front of the restaurant when the door flew open and a pair of cowboys strode outside and nearly walked right over him.

They were two young men with full bellies and the arrogant confidence that marked most of their type. Looking over at Clint, they put on an expression as though they hoped he would throw an insult in their direction so they could work off their meal.

Clint held back a smirk and stepped aside for them to

walk on by while keeping their pride intact.

"Keep steppin', mister," the smaller of the two said. "You got two boys from the Homes spread coming through."

After all he'd been through and with the hunger starting to twist inside his stomach, Clint wasn't in the mood for the cocky stares and puffed chests of the two who stopped to look him over.

Obviously the one with more to prove, the smaller one stopped and faced Clint. "You're standing in our way, old man. Didn't you hear who you're dealing with?"

Since neither of the cowboys were about to let him walk through the door quietly, Clint locked eyes with the spokesman of the pair and said, "I heard who you are and that name doesn't mean a damn thing to me. So why don't you save the tough talk for the saloon where you've got some ladies to impress?"

Clint's tone was cool and deadly as the edge of a Bowie knife. It obviously had an effect on the kid, but he quickly tried to recover. His eyes flashed with a mix of both anger and uncertainty as his hand dropped to the gun at his side. "You want to finish this, then you can come find us at the saloon right down th—"

The kid stopped in mid-threat when he saw a flicker of motion at the very bottom of his field of vision. When he looked down, he spotted Clint's hand was full of a modified Colt pointed directly at his gut. The kid's own hand had barely pulled the gun halfway from his holster. Clint was angry enough that he had broken a lifelong rule never to draw his gun unless he was going to use it.

"I've had a long couple of days," Clint said evenly. "I'm hungry and all I want is a steak. You and your friend can go to your saloon, have your drinks, and brag to your buddies because as far as this little dance goes, it's finished." Slowly turning his eyes to the kid's bigger companion, Clint added, "And trust me, junior, you'd best put those bad looks away before someone not as patient as I am blows them off both your skulls."

Clint kept his eyes on the two for another couple of seconds while his words sunk in. Before too long, the smaller kid dropped his gun back into his holster and took a step back.

"Why don't you both take those gun belts off," Clint said. "I'll make sure the town's law gets them."

Like two spoiled children, the cowboys' first reaction was to protest, but they thought better of it in less than a second. Muttering under their breaths, they unbuckled their holsters and let them drop to the boards at their feet.

Clint holstered his pistol as well and gave the cowboys a wide smile. "So how's the steak in there?"

The smaller one opened his mouth to say something, but his bigger friend stopped him with a hand on his shoulder. By the look on the short one's face, he wasn't about to say anything too good.

"Probably a safe move there, partner," Clint said to the cowboy who'd stopped the shorter one from talking.

"Come on," the taller of the two said. "Let's get the hell out of here."

TEN

Shaking his head, Clint watched the cowboys turn away and walk down to the street. In less than four or five paces, the two had already regained their cocky struts and were joking loudly to anyone who would listen. He reached down to scoop up the pair of holsters and slung them over his shoulder. When he turned back toward the steakhouse, Clint found himself face to face with a woman that damn near took the breath right out of him.

The woman standing in the doorway had blonde hair that flowed freely around her face, framed a set of striking blue eyes and brushed against the sides of her large, rounded breasts. "Get yourself in here," she said.

Clint was stricken for a moment by the sheer contrast of looking at her after dealing with the two cowboys and thinking about a corpse for the last several days. "Excuse me?"

Her lips were wide and shaped almost like the bow on top of a Christmas present. They looked even more attractive when they curved up into a beaming smile. "I saw what happened out here. After the way you put those two in their place, I figure you earned yourself a free meal."

Now it was Clint's turn to smile and he did so even wider when he saw the blonde woman hold out her arms invitingly. "Well, this just keeps getting better," he said while starting to walk forward into her waiting embrace.

Already smiling, the blonde took half a step back and laughed just a little bit. "Don't get too excited just yet. But I'll surely take those guns to the sheriff if you like."

Clint felt his cheeks flush and he handed over the holsters. "Can't blame a man for keeping his hopes up."

"Not at all," she said with a friendly wink. "And there's no reason to lose those hopes, either. Come on inside and take a seat. I'll be with you as soon as I drop these off somewhere safe."

Stepping into the restaurant, Clint was immediately wrapped up in the enticing aromas that had drawn him there in the first place. To make things seem even better, he got a look at the blonde as she turned and walked toward a counter just inside the door. Her hips shifted back and forth beneath her skirt in a way that kept Clint's attention until she disappeared into another room next to the kitchen.

Once she was gone, Clint allowed himself to turn back toward the dining room and look around for an empty chair. The place seemed to be doing pretty good business. Now that he'd gotten to smell the food and see one of the women who worked there, Clint didn't have any question as to where so many customers would come from.

Still mostly full, the dining room was bustling with activity and filled with the noise of so many conversations all blending into one. Most of the occupied tables were in front of or close to a pair of picture windows looking out onto the street. Although that might have been the best view in the place, Clint preferred to have his back to a solid wall and walked toward a table near the rear of the restaurant.

Clint's table was big enough to seat four, but had only one chair propped against it. He dragged the chair around until he was facing the rest of the room and had a seat. By the time his backside was pressed fully against the surface of the chair, Clint spotted the gorgeous blonde emerging from the adjoining room.

The smile appeared instantly on her face as she made her way through the room. Judging by the looks on the male faces as she walked by, they might have been regulars, but they were still taken in by their host. She exchanged friendly words with nearly everyone she passed, all the while making her way to Clint's table in the back.

Without breaking stride, she took hold of an empty chair by the backrest and moved it so she could sit close enough to touch Clint's hand, but still far enough away so her closeness wouldn't be considered intimate. "If you wanted to eat alone, I could just—"

"You could just stop what you were about to say because I wouldn't mind having some company at all," Clint interrupted.

The blonde nodded once and pulled her chair a little closer. "Great. My name is Pamela Caudry."

"Clint Adams. Are you the hostess here?"

"Hostess and owner."

"You mean there isn't a Pappy around here somewhere?"

By the way she rolled her eyes, that wasn't the first time she'd heard that particular statement. "Not unless you count my father. He was the one responsible for the name of this place originally, but not like you think. He put up the initial investment so I could open this place, but on one condition.

"He called me Pammy ever since I was a little girl and wanted that to be name of the restaurant."

Clint couldn't help but cringe. "Pammy's? That sounds like a couple things, but a steakhouse isn't one of them."

"I know, I know. It wasn't until he heard someone ask why I would open a brothel that my father finally gave in on the whole name issue. After a month or so, I didn't have enough money for a whole new sign so I painted over a few letters and things took off from there."

"I'll bet it makes a world of difference once folks aren't afraid to bring their families in here, huh?"

Her laughter wasn't exactly musical, but it wasn't the forced kind that usually came out of most hostesses Clint had met. She smoothed her hair back away from her face and said, "Yes. That certainly did help. So what can I get for you?"

"I'll take one of Pappy's steaks, of course. I'm awful hungry, so you might want to reconsider that offer of a free meal, because it might wind up costing you."

"Please. I've been trying to get those two to stop from coming around here for weeks, but haven't had any luck."

Clint let his eyes wander over Pamela's face before drifting lower. Her skin was smooth and slightly bronzed from the sun. The neckline of her dress was cut low enough to display her ample cleavage and the material clung to her body. "There's no doubt in my mind that you'd have a hard time getting those two boys to leave you alone."

She dropped her eyes from his for a second and then looked back up again. "Seeing them backed down like that was fun. Knowing that they'll steer clear for a little bit is worth a lot more than a steak dinner."

"Are you offering me dessert as well?"

"Most definitely."

"Then let's get started. If I have to smell that steak cooking any more without tasting some for myself, I'd have to accuse you of torturing a man to death."

"Coming right up," she said while pushing away from the table and getting to her feet. "I'll get you the biggest cut we have along with a baked potato and some greens. How does that sound?"

"I'm sold."

"I'll let the cook know and then I'll be back with something to drink. I don't serve alcohol, so how about some coffee instead?"

"Sounds good." Actually, since he'd been hitting the bottom of his personal food stores, Clint had been brewing nothing but old beans and used grinds the last couple mornings on the trail. Fresh coffee sounded like an answer to his prayers.

"I'll be right back."

Watching her walk away, Clint damn near forgot what had brought him into Estes Canyon to begin with. He preferred to keep it that way for the moment. At least he could enjoy his meal without letting those morbid questions start flowing through his head all over again.

Perhaps things would seem clearer once he had a full stomach.

ELEVEN

Clint took one bite from the thick cut of meat that was placed in front of him and instantly felt like a criminal. "Oh my lord," he said through a mouthful of partially chewed beef.

Nodding, Pamela said, "I know. That's the family specialty you're tasting."

Savoring every second as he chewed, Clint was already slicing off another piece as he swallowed. "You've got to let me pay for this. This is too good for you to just give it away."

"Another man told me that once before he even walked into my restaurant. Of course, that's when everyone was still under the impression that I was running a cathouse and I don't think he was talking about the steak."

Clint laughed, but didn't let himself be distracted from his knife and fork. "I'll just leave that comment alone before I talk myself out of the best supper I've had in a month of Sundays."

"Nah. I doubt you could say anything worse than those two who you chased away from here."

"They were just young and full of steam. I took their guns to keep them from hurting themselves more than anything else." The bite of steak melted in Clint's mouth, but he couldn't ignore the rest of his plate any longer.

There was a heaping pile of greens next to a baked potato that was split down the middle and covered with melted butter and sour cream.

Cutting off a piece of the potato, Clint sopped up some of the juices from the steak and popped it into his mouth. The combination of flavors was enough to make him shake his head again and consider actually praising the chain of events that had brought him to that particular restaurant.

As if reading his mind, Pamela asked, "So do you have business in town or are you just passing through?"

That single question brought all of the things that Clint had been trying to forget about back to the front of his mind. Those recent memories were almost enough to take away some of the pleasure he was getting from his meal.

Almost, but not quite.

Clint swallowed his food and washed it down with a sip of hot coffee. "I was intending on passing through this area, but wound up taking on a bit of business along the way."

"Is that so? What kind of business?"

Clint's first impulse was to describe a bit of the grisly details that had brought him to town, if only just to see if Pamela's reaction would give him anything to work with. But rather than repay her hospitality with a description of a mutilated corpse, Clint shrugged and said, "I found a runaway horse that might belong to someone from around here." Although he'd opted against disclosing every last detail, he was still watching her for a reaction.

"I don't know anyone who lost a horse. Maybe you should ask the sheriff when you see him. Were you still planning on talking to him after you ate?"

"Most likely."

"Good. Because I'm sure you'll come up in conversation once those two boys from the Homes spread get drunk and start flapping their gums at that saloon they practically live at." She thought for a second and took a sip of her own coffee. "How do you know the horse came from here?"

"Let's just say I was certain the horse wasn't wild, so I looked through the saddlebags for something that might tell me about the owner."

Nodding and leaning forward as though she was listening to a mystery story, Pamela held her coffee in both hands so the steam drifted up into her face. "Yeah? And what did you find?"

As much as he liked Pamela's company and appreciated the kindness she'd shown him, Clint forced himself to hold back a bit before opening up to her completely. She seemed like a nice enough person, but whatever had happened to the man he'd found tied to that horse was a whole lot of bad business. Whoever would do such a thing would surely be on the lookout for someone who'd found out about it. At the very least, they surely wouldn't appreciate the fact that anyone was checking back in on them.

Clint had been watching Pamela closely and so far hadn't seen anything but natural curiosity from her. All the same, he figured it was still best to keep things safe for the time being.

"There wasn't a whole lot in the bags," he said after cutting into his steak. "Just some pictures and a letter that was addressed to a woman in Estes Canyon."

"What's her name? If she's lived here for any amount of time, I probably know her. I've probably even served her a meal or two."

Studying her without making it appear that way, Clint looked up and said, "Bonnie Shaughnessey. You know her?"

Without the slightest hesitation, Pamela nodded. "Sure, I know Bonnie. I didn't know she was missing a horse, though. And I thought all of her family was either here in town or the next town over. Was the name of the person who sent the letter written on it anywhere?"

"If I saw that, I wouldn't have to ask about whose horse that was, now would I?"

"No, I suppose not," Pamela said, looking slightly embarrassed. "That was a silly question."

"Actually, I didn't open the letter. It just didn't seem right."

When Pamela looked at him, she was smiling again. "That's admirable, Clint. Most men would've read that letter while riding the horse off to be sold somewhere or just take it for themselves. Not only do you bring it back without looking into someone else's things, but you come here to help me with my little rat problem as well."

"And just in time for dinner. Don't forget that part."

Her smile widened and she reached out once again to place her hand upon Clint's. "I'm glad you came here when you did, Clint."

"So am I. This night's turned out better than I could have hoped." Clint might have been good at keeping a good poker face, but even a blind man would have been able to see that, just then, he wasn't referring to the steak.

TWELVE

As the sun dropped lower in the sky, the people wandering the streets of Estes Canyon started moving away from one end of town and headed for another. Like a flock of birds going through their daily migration, locals and visitors alike left the business district in favor of the more social locations three streets away.

Except for the occasional straggler, nearly every sign of life the town had to offer was either indoors or kicking up their heels at one of the town's saloons or cathouses. For that reason, the pair of figures walking away from the drinking district and heading toward the restaurant seemed like birds breaking out of formation.

They stuck out like sore thumbs as they crossed the street and went straight to the boardwalk in front of the steakhouse. One of the men was obviously younger than the other. This was clear not so much by the way he looked, but by the way he moved. For every step the other man took, the first one took three. In fact, he seemed to be doing everything but literally running circles around the other, wildly gesturing with his hands while speaking in a rushed stream of syllables.

As the younger man walked and talked, he nervously glanced from side to side, all the while pointing toward the steakhouse. He was dressed in clothes that marked him as a cowboy, just as he'd been dressed when he had met up with Clint Adams not too long ago in front of that same restaurant.

The older man was dressed in a crisply pressed and perfectly tailored black suit. He strode with absolute confidence that only came with age and success. Every part of him reeked of money, starting with the silk suit, running down to the silver-tipped walking stick in his hand and going all the way down to the boots that were polished well enough to reflect starlight back up into the sky.

Although the younger man was physically bigger than the gentleman, he kept his back stooped and his head low as if deferring to the other figure. His steps were quick, yet shuffling, and made almost as much noise as his chattering voice.

"It's right over there," the younger man said. "I told you it was there and you can see it. See it?"

"Yeah, I see it," the gentleman said while batting away the other guy's hand like he was swatting a fly. "How long's it been there?"

"I don't know. We were just coming out after eating dinner and we ran into this fella. Damn near ran straight over him and then—"

"Let me guess. Kyle started running off at the mouth and got himself slapped in the face like a woman?"

"No!" was the first, reflexive thing from the younger man's mouth. After a quick reconsideration, he shrugged and said, "Well . . . sort of. But that's when I got a look at that."

They'd come to a stop in front of the steakhouse and the taller of the two cowboys that Clint had encountered earlier was now pointing toward the horses tied to the hitching post. The well-dressed gentleman sauntered over to the horse next to the black Darley Arabian and looked it over as though he was interested in making an offer to buy it.

"That's the one, isn't it?" the younger man asked. "That's the horse, Mister Homes, I'd swear to it."

When he looked up at the cowboy, Homes stared into his eyes for just a second. The look was more of a way to get the guy to calm down than anything meant to threaten him. The gentleman's features were smooth, yet handsome. A thin mustache grew over his lip and was clipped neatly before it could make it over the corners of his mouth.

"Yeah," Homes said. "That's the bastard's horse, all right."

"I knew it!"

Homes's stare became a warning glare, forcing the cowboy to lose some of the enthusiasm that had suddenly flooded into him.

"Shut yer mouth, Tom, before you call out the whole damn town."

"Sorry, Mister Homes. But I knew that was the horse. I knew it the moment I saw it standing there."

"Great. You knew it. Splendid. Now tell me you know how it got tied to this post and I'll be impressed."

Tom started to say something, but cut himself short when he took a moment to think about what was about to come out of his mouth. Rather than let himself blurt out the first thing he was going to say, he lowered his head and finally calmed himself down.

"No?" Homes said, lowering his gaze so he could still see the younger man's eyes. "I didn't think so. Can you find out who found this animal or do I have to find someone more capable?"

"I can find out, Mister Homes. I already seen the man who it had to be. I met him face to face."

"But can you keep from making an ass out of yourself like your friend Kyle?"

Tom nodded intently as though he just then realized he wasn't supposed to be carrying on.

"Just get me his name and his business here," Homes instructed. "Pry any further than that and he'll probably shoot a hole through you."

With the thought of his last encounter in front of that restaurant still fresh in his mind, Tom knew better than to try and argue against Homes's point. Instead, he nodded and started walking up the steps toward the steakhouse. Reluctantly, he put his hand on the door handle, waited, and finally pulled it open to walk inside.

Homes watched the entire time, amused by the younger man. Tom acted as though he was going to war or taking on some kind of mission for his country. All he wanted was a name and the same amount of information the stranger might give in a casual conversation. Was that so much to ask? Well, judging by the look on the younger man's face, it might just be.

The well-dressed gentleman shook his head and started walking toward the saloon where he knew Tom's friend would be. There wasn't any need to worry just yet. After all, this stranger might have just found the horse and was going to drop it off. If there was anything more than that going on, then it would be the stranger who needed to worry.

THIRTEEN

For dessert, Pamela didn't even ask Clint what he wanted. Instead, she'd waited until he was about done with his meal, excused herself for a moment, and came back with a smaller plate, which she sat in front of him.

"What's this?" Clint asked while dabbing at his mouth with a napkin.

"Another one of my specialties. Try some if you've still got any room after devouring that steak."

By the time she'd finished her sentence, the scent came up from the plate and drifted into Clint's nose. It was hot apple pie and even though he'd been reaching the limits of what his stomach could hold, Clint wasn't about to turn away from something that smelled that good.

"It's my aunt's recipe," Pamela said when Clint sectioned off a piece with his fork and lifted it to his mouth.

The dessert was almost too hot for him to eat, but after a few cooling breaths, the flavor sank into his tongue. At that moment, Clint knew why Pamela had opened up a steakhouse and not a bakery. There wasn't anything wrong with the pie, but perhaps it just paled in comparison to what he'd eaten before. It was good enough that he didn't have to fake the smile on his face.

"You like it?" she asked.

"I sure do. But I probably won't be able to eat all of it."

Scooting her chair in a little closer, Pamela took the fork from Clint's hand and sliced off a small bite for herself. She didn't take her eyes off of him as she closed her lips around the apple and crust and eased the fork out between her fingers. A spark passed between them as she finished her bite and handed the fork back over to him. "Hope you don't mind if I give you a little help."

"Not at all." When Clint used that fork to take another bite of pie, he could taste the subtle hint of what could only be Pamela's lips mixed in with the rest. The flavor was sweet and reminded Clint of a kiss. Suddenly, he couldn't think about much else besides what the rest of her would taste like.

Between the both of them, they polished off the pie without much trouble at all. When Clint sat back to make it easier for the rest of his food to go down, he noticed a familiar face toward the front of the restaurant. The place had cleared out considerably as he'd eaten, but there were still a few occupied tables. His eyes focused on the table closest to the door, however, and when he looked at the man sitting there, Tom immediately looked away.

"Looks like I didn't do as good a job as I thought," he said.

When Pamela looked at him questioningly, Clint motioned his eyes toward the table that had caught his attention. Pamela didn't try to hide her movement at all when she twisted in her chair to look in the direction Clint had shown her.

She only had to look for a second before she saw Tom sitting there with his head down and his hands folded around the glass of water he'd ordered. "Jesus, what's he doing here?" She groaned, while turning back around to face Clint. "After you scared off his friend I thought that one would know better than to come around here again. Maybe he'll just get bored and leave."

Clint stood up and was about to walk over there when he stopped and lowered himself back into his seat. "Or maybe he knows how to take a hint better than his buddy."

Once again, Pamela turned around to look for herself and was pleased to see Tom push away from his table and head straight for the door. She kept her eyes on the door for a few seconds after he left as though she was waiting for the cowboy to come charging back inside.

"That's odd," she said with a shrug. "I'm glad to see him go, but that's still awful strange."

"Could be he just wanted to prove he wasn't too scared to come back in here. Hell, it might have been the little one who dared him to drop by." Although neither of those two possibilities were very possible, Clint doubted it could be anything so simple. Partly because he could smell the fear coming off both of those two cowboys and it was enough to keep them away for some time. Also, Clint had been around too long to expect anything to be simple.

Those possibilities seemed to satisfy Pamela, however, which was all Clint had really been hoping for.

"You're probably right," she said, settling into her seat with her back to the rest of the room. "Now, what were we talking about?"

"Well, I was just about to ask if you knew a good place in town where I could rent a room."

"There's rooms to be rented in a saloon not too far from here. If you don't mind spending a bit more, there's a nice little hotel a block away that serves a good breakfast. I go there myself sometimes when I get sick of eating here."

"After spending so much time on the trail, I don't mind spending a little extra just so long as the beds are soft."

Pamela's smile widened just a little bit when Clint mentioned a bed. He could tell that she tried to hide the grin, but he'd seen just enough. "Before I head out of here, though, I'd like to ask you another question."

Her eyes widening a bit, Pamela straightened up as though she'd just remembered something important. "Oh! Of course. Bonnie Shaughnessey. I can tell you where to find her and even let her know you're coming if you'd like."

"An introduction would be nice. There's also something else, if you have the time. It's just a little something."

Reaching out to pat his hand, Pamela said, "Don't worry. I wasn't planning on leaving you alone just yet."

Clint had already been reaching into his jacket pocket and when he took his hand out, he was holding the bundle of pictures he'd found on the dead man's body. Heaving already rearranged the pictures before riding into town, Clint unfolded them and placed the stack upon the table with the photograph of the two women staring up at Pamela.

"Do you know these two women?" he asked.

When she looked down at the photograph, the smile on Pamela's face dimmed like the flame of a dying candle. It was still there, but mostly as an afterthought without any of the feeling that had been inside it before. "Well, the dark-haired girl is Bonnie."

Watching Pamela as closely as he could without making her nervous, Clint asked, "What about the blonde?"

"That's Luanne Parkinson."

"Does she live around here?"

"Yes, she does."

"You don't seem to like her too much."

"Well, I'd rather talk about other things besides liars and whores, so if you want to know all about Luanne, you can talk to some of the trash in town that also spread their legs for a living."

"All right," Clint said while sweeping up the pictures, refolding them and slipping them back into his pocket. He didn't show her the picture of the man, because if she knew him it might be a shock. "Instead of that, why don't I buy you a drink? It's the least I can do after that steak you gave me."

Pamela's smile brightened noticeably, but it wasn't back to 100 percent. She seemed happy enough once the picture was out of her sight and Clint was ready to escort her outside.

FOURTEEN

Tom could feel his heart beating like a drum inside his chest. At first, he'd been nervous that Mister Homes would be outside to see when he came from the restaurant like a dog with his tail between his legs. Although the well-dressed man was nowhere to be seen, Tom felt his nerves act up again once he decided to start poking through the bags on the stranger's horse to see if he could find something to salvage the mess he'd made of his job.

The moment he laid hands on the saddlebags, Tom felt the stallion shift and fidget from one foot to another. Not only did the Darley Arabian seem anxious, but it even turned its head to snort at him as though warning him to back away.

Tom wasn't the type to be frightened by a horse, but the animal's behavior acted right alongside the nervousness he'd already been feeling, which caused him to instinctively back up. He felt foolish the moment he moved back and so he started reaching out a second time for the leather bags.

Just when he was getting his confidence back and was feeling superior to the dumb animal in front of him, Tom pulled his hand back again as Eclipse turned and nearly bit off two of his fingers. Cursing under his breath, he held onto his hand and was glad just to feel that it was all still there.

"Dammit," he hissed. "Goddamn horse."

Eclipse was already dipping his nose back into the trough next to the hitching post. The muscles under the stallion's black coat were more tense than normal however, as he seemed to be ready for the next time Tom would try to steal from those bags.

Standing in place, Tom considered if he should take another go at those bags. The door to the restaurant opened behind him, causing him to nearly trip over himself while trying to look casual to whomever was stepping outside.

Thankfully, it wasn't the stranger leaving the restaurant. Tom shot the local man and woman a mean look that sped the couple along their way, leaving him once again alone with the two horses. Looking at those saddlebags, Tom thought he could hear a clock ticking away the seconds that he'd already wasted trying to get at the damn things. Plus, still holding onto his hand was enough to remind him of what else might happen if he made another attempt.

Giving the horses a wide berth, Tom walked around them so he could look into the picture windows on the front of the steakhouse. He kept himself mostly in the street, which left him outside of most of the light that spilled out from the restaurant. From there, he was able to get a look inside the place.

He didn't see much, but he was able to make out the shape of Pamela Caudry sitting next to that stranger, talking to him like he was something special. That sight alone was enough to make Tom's eyes narrow and a scowl crawl over his lips.

Like most every other healthy man in Estes Canyon, Tom had thought more than once about what it would be like to garner some of Pamela's favor. When he saw her smiling at the stranger after he'd only been in town for an hour or so, Tom damn near pulled his gun and started shooting through the window.

At that moment, Tom realized that he didn't even have his gun any longer, thanks to that same son of a bitch sitting inside the steakhouse. That only made Tom madder. He was so mad, in fact, that when he saw Pamela and the stranger get up and head for the door, he didn't make a move right away to get out of the street.

"Let him come," Tom thought in a red haze. "That son of a bitch thinks he's so much, let him come outside and prove it."

All of that anger felt fine and good right up until the stranger casually glanced outside and stopped as though he'd spotted Tom through the window.

The instant Tom thought he was staring directly into Clint's face, he could only think of getting out of the street as quickly as his legs could carry him. No amount of anger could make him forget the sight of that stranger drawing his pistol on Kyle earlier.

Actually, what put the scare into Tom was the fact that he hadn't been able to see the stranger draw his gun. At least that made him feel a little less cowardly when he found himself hightailing it to the alley next to the steakhouse.

The door opened and Tom could hear footsteps clomping along the boardwalk and then making their way down the steps to the street. He listened to the voices that accompanied those footsteps and immediately recognized the ones belonging to first Pamela and then the stranger.

They still seemed to be getting along pretty good, which only served to make Tom's blood boil. He held his ground in the shadows as the couple walked by. Once he was looking at them from behind, Tom shaped his fingers into a gun, pointed it at the back of Clint's head, and pulled his imaginary trigger.

FIFTEEN

"You look tired," Pamela said as she strolled beside Clint down the side of the street.

It was too dark to see the name of the street they were on, but Clint was certain he could find his way around the town easily enough if he just kept his eyes open. He looked around at first for a street sign, but soon found himself simply admiring the view.

"I don't feel tired," Clint said while still looking up at the blanket of shimmering stars over his head. Turning to look at Pamela, he asked, "Or are you just trying to get out of me taking you for that drink?"

"Nothing of the sort. Actually, I was just checking to see if you might want to settle in at your hotel first before going to a saloon."

Suddenly, Clint stopped and turned around. It took a little quick maneuvering, but Pamela's reflexes were good enough for her to stay with him.

"What's wrong?" she asked, while trying to see what he was looking at. "What is it, Clint?"

"My horse. I need to get him put up for the night before I go off and do much of anything else."

"Can't he wait?"

Clint looked at her and was captivated by the way the night had turned Pamela's eyes into the deep blue of nighttime waters. She looked back at him as well, telling him a whole lot about the way his evening might turn out.

"Actually, I think I'd better see to him before I get more distracted than I already am."

"Fine. There's a good livery that's at the other end of this street. The owners live in the house right next to it so you should be able to get them even at this hour."

Clint was turning to look back at Eclipse when something else caught his eye. There was just a strange way one of the shadows shifted that made him stop before shifting his gaze any farther.

Placing one hand on his shoulder, Pamela looked over at him and then tried to follow his line of sight. "What's wrong, Clint? You look like—"

He stopped her with a quickly raised index finger, not taking his eyes from where they were. After she'd quieted down, Clint lowered his finger until he was pointing toward the alley next to Pappy's Steakhouse. He could tell that she was looking that way, too, focusing in on the darkness even though she wasn't exactly sure what to look for.

Keeping his voice low enough so that only she could hear him, Clint said, "Stay here."

Pamela wanted to go with him, if only to see what could be happening so close to her business, but the intensity in Clint's voice rooted her to the spot. At least, it kept her still until he was halfway to the alley.

As he walked toward the dark opening between the steakhouse and its neighbor, Clint could see another bit of movement that was even more pronounced than the one that had first caught his attention. There was a sound as well, which sounded like boots scraping against the dirt.

After only a few steps, Clint could see that the shadow he'd spotted was most definitely a person standing in the darkness, trying not to be seen. As he started moving quickly toward it, however, that figure turned and was starting to make a move. By the sound of the footsteps, the figure was running but because of the darkness, it was hard for Clint to see if the person was coming or going.

Not wanting to butt heads with someone running directly at him, Clint eased up for a second and let his hand drop toward his gun. In the next second, it became obvious the figure was actually running away rather than coming straight at him.

Clint ran a few paces, but the other person had gotten too much of a head start and ducked around a corner before Clint was a quarter of the way into the narrow walkway. Rather than put all of his steam into pursuing the shadowy figure, Clint eased up and turned around. His hand wrapped around the Colt's handle out of pure reflex when he found himself face to face with someone that had been standing directly behind him.

"Jesus, Pamela, you just about got yourself killed," Clint said before he could stop himself.

Although she looked a little shocked by the speed of his gun hand, she didn't seem offended by his harsh tone. "Sorry, but I thought you might need some help." Craning her neck to try and look past him into the alley, she asked, "Who was that?"

"I don't know. It could've just been some kid sneaking around for all I know."

"Whoever he was, he sure was fast."

"Yeah. He was, at that. This stable that's open all hours . . . is it safe?"

Pamela smirked and nodded. "Anyone who goes near that barn without the owner's say-so gets an ass full of buckshot."

"I like the sound of that. Why don't I meet you after I get my animals squared away?"

"All right. After I close up my restaurant, I can scout ahead and arrange for your room. Like I said, I know the owners, so I should be able to get you some kind of deal on the price."

"Sounds good." Truth be told, Clint was glad to just get himself and the horses away from Pamela and her place of business. Something in his gut told him that there was some trouble brewing around him regarding the matter that had brought him into Estes Canyon. If it was going to follow him around, he figured he'd best make sure it wasn't too close before he bedded down for the night. Once the horses were put up and the saddlebags were off their backs, he figured anyone poking around would probably lose interest in them as well.

It was obvious that Pamela knew something was bothering Clint. She watched him carefully as he stepped out of the alley. Her eyes drifted down toward the gun at his side and though she seemed a little put off by the sight of it, she seemed a little excited to see it there as well. Her excitement wasn't anything too noticeable, just a flush in her cheeks and a widening of her eyes.

"The place I was going to see about for you is called the Canyon Inn," she said. "It's at the end of Main Street, at the other edge of town."

"I'll be there as soon as I can. Thanks for the help."

As she headed toward the steakhouse, Pamela stopped and said, "I hope you're not so distracted when you do show up. If I were you, I wouldn't worry too much. Those two aren't the types to cause trouble on someone they know will fight back."

With the little scuffle he'd had in front of the restaurant pushed to the back of his mind, Clint had to think for a moment as to what she was talking about. The faces of those two cowboys came back into his head, which jogged another memory loose as well. "I'm not worried," he said with a smile. "Just a bit worn out, that's all."

Pamela turned and stepped into her restaurant, shutting the door behind her.

The other memory that Clint had recalled was when he and Pamela had been about to leave the steakhouse just a couple minutes ago. After getting up out of his seat, he thought he'd spotted someone through the window, staring in from the street. The figure moved out of sight before Clint could get too suspicious and not too long after that, he'd seen another figure watching him from the shadows of an alley.

He had no way of knowing if that person in the alley had been anyone sinister or just someone out for a look-see. The more he thought about it, though, the more he started letting those questions drift through his brain again.

Although he didn't have anything against mixing a little bit of pleasure in with his business, Clint reminded himself once again that he might just be getting himself into some very dangerous business indeed.

Things always tended to get messy when killing was involved, but Clint was used to that. It was amazing what a man could get himself used to.

SIXTEEN

Clint had actually been happy to see the old man greet him before he'd led Eclipse and the other horse up to the livery stable. He'd made it to about ten feet from knocking distance of the door when a bulky man wearing nothing but a nightshirt and boots came thundering out of the nearby house.

"Who the hell are you?" the old man shouted, his mouth moving unseen behind a thick layer of wiry beard. His question was punctuated by the snap of both triggers of a shotgun being pulled back as the weapon was aimed in Clint's direction.

Holding his hands up, Clint stayed right where he was. "I'm just here to drop off these horses. I take it you run this livery?"

Peering at him from beneath thick brows, the old man relaxed only slightly as he took a step forward. "I ain't seen you before."

"New in town just this evening. I need to put these horses up where they'll be safe. I think someone might be out to steal one or both of them."

"I ain't surprised. It's been a coon's age since I set eyes on a Darley Arabian as fine as that one. But that other one . . ." His words trailed off and every one of his muscles tensed. The shotgun snapped up to his shoulder and he stared at Clint down along the barrel. "That's Jack MacFarlane's horse you got there!"

Clint hadn't seen that one coming, although he probably should have guessed the owner of a livery would have a good eye for horses. Just another way for Clint to see how much of a toll the day had taken on him.

"Jack MacFarlane?" Clint asked. "You know him?"

"He lived here, but you would'a known that if you came by that there horse honestly. I'll wager you stole that other one as well."

"I didn't steal this horse. I was bringing it back. I found it."

"Sure you did. Toss down them reins and your gun as well."

Clint dropped the reins he'd been holding, but kept his hands in the air without making a move toward his Colt. "Like I said, I came here to put these animals up for the night. You can take them, but only because I'll pay you for a stall. My gun stays with me."

The old man shook his head. "Where I come from, horse thieves swing from a noose. You'll toss down that pistol or I'll empty both barrels into you and claim the reward that's probably on your head."

Every one of Clint's senses were taking in the old man. He watched every move and listened to every sound. More importantly, he used senses that had been honed after years of observing people. A man wasn't born with those kind of senses. He had to sharpen them over the years like he was dragging a blade over a whetstone until he got a razor edge.

Observing the old man like that, Clint could tell two things right off the bat. First of all, the man didn't want to pull the triggers on that shotgun. Second, the old man would kill him if he was pushed far enough.

"When was the last time you saw this Jack Mac-Farlane?" Clint asked.

"About four days ago. And he was on that horse."

"Was he in any trouble?"

"What do you mean by asking all these questions? You'll throw down that pistol or you'll die! Jack Mac-Farlane was a friend of mine."

"Then help me find out who killed him."

That caused the old man to pause for a second. His breath caught in his throat, causing him to choke on what he'd been about to say. After another second, the old man glared intently into Clint's eyes. "He's dead?"

Knowing that the old man was now studying him with the same amount of intensity, Clint nodded. "I found him on that horse and brought him back here to see what happened."

"How would you know to come here unless he told you where he was from?"

"I found a letter in his pocket. It was addressed to someone living here." Reaching slowly for his jacket, Clint said, "If you let me, I can show you the letter I'm talking about."

After thinking it over for a second or two, the old man tilted his head slightly so he could take better aim. "If you make one move for that gun, I'll shoot. Believe me on that, mister."

"I believe you." But Clint's hand went nowhere near his holster. Luckily, he'd put the letter back into the breast pocket of his jacket and he got the paper out without tempting the old man's trigger finger. "Here. Take a look for yourself."

"Toss it to me."

Clint snapped his wrist and sent the paper flying. It landed a few inches from the liveryman's feet.

The old man squatted down to pick up the paper, keeping the shotgun trained on Clint the entire time. He had to hold the letter up close to his face so he could read it and when he did, his eyes widened. Turning it over, he looked at the wax seal. "You didn't open it."

"No," Clint said. "It's not addressed to me."

"I can't say for certain, but this looks like Jack's writing. He always did scribble like he was runnin' for president." Focusing all of his attention on Clint, he said, "Most thieves I know would've read this and probably burned it in their campfire."

"True," Clint said. "And most killers would have shot you while you were staring at that letter."

The old man straightened up and swallowed hard, realizing the truth in Clint's observation. Still looking down the barrel of his shotgun, the old man tossed the letter back and lowered the hammers. "I'll take them horses, but Jack's ain't goin' nowhere until I get some answers."

"Fine with me. How much do I owe you?"

"I'll be tellin' the sheriff as well. So if you're lying I'll get my payment when I see you swing. If you're tellin' the truth about finding Jack and wanting to get who done it, then I couldn't see my way clear to chargin' you a dime. Like I said, Jack was my friend."

Clint nodded and slowly lowered his hands. When he saw that the old man wasn't going to raise his shotgun again, he said, "I'll be staying at the Canyon Inn if you want to get a hold of me. Otherwise, I'd like to talk to you tomorrow about Jack MacFarlane."

Still studying Clint carefully, the old man moved forward until he was close enough to pick up the reins that Clint had thrown down. He was also well within Clint's reach when he stooped down to snatch up the leather straps.

"That's twice you didn't try to get the jump on me when you had the chance," the liveryman pointed out. "I'm old enough to follow my gut and it's tellin' me to give you the benefit of the doubt for now."

"I appreciate that."

"Well, don't let it get to your head. I'm also ornery

enough to make good on my promise to see you dead if you're playing me for a fool."

Once again, Clint showed the old man the palms of both his hands. "You don't have to convince me. I'm just glad someone like you is looking after those animals."

Although the old man still didn't seem to know quite what to make of him, he nodded at Clint and shuffled backward to the stable. Both horses followed him without question. All the while, the old man kept both eyes intently on Clint.

"And I'll be tellin' the sheriff about this," the liveryman repeated. "He'll find you no matter where you run."

Clint laughed a little, but more at the situation instead of at the old man. "The only place I'll be running is to the Canyon Inn." With that, he turned around and walked away from the stable. Once he was back at the side of the street, he glanced back to check on the old man.

Eclipse and the other horse were being shown into the stable and the shotgun had already been propped up against the side of that building. From where he was, Clint could hear the old man grumbling to himself as if complaining to some invisible helper.

The old-timer might have had a loose screw or two, but he seemed reliable enough. Clint had to laugh once again at the fact that he not only liked the man who'd held him at gunpoint and threatened to watch him hang, but was inclined to trust him as well.

SEVENTEEN

Following the directions Pamela had given him, Clint had no trouble whatsoever finding the Canyon Inn. It seemed the place was set up to attract the eye of anyone entering town from the west, so that made things a bit easier as well. The building was two floors high and was only slightly wider than any of the other storefronts, but was noticeably fancier than anything in the immediate vicinity.

The sign over its front porch was bigger than the front window and written in flowing letters with paint so fresh it seemed to glow in the dark. Also, there was a light in every one of the windows facing the street, which attracted Clint's eyes even more.

When he stepped inside the lobby, Clint thought he might have made a mistake and walked into a saloon instead. There was a small bar with three or four tables scattered around as well as a piano set against the farthest wall. Only one of the tables was full, but there wasn't a single place to stand at the bar.

"Can I help you?" came a voice from Clint's left.

Turning to look and see who was talking, Clint spotted a balding man in his late thirties wearing a plain white shirt and suspenders holding up black trousers. The man stood leaning over the side of the bar, stretching his neck out like a turtle so he could hear Clint's reply.

"Actually I need a room," Clint said.

"Sure 'nuff. Just give me a second."

In fact, a second was all the man needed as he all but vaulted over the bar and rushed to Clint's side. Motioning with his hand, he said, "Follow me, sir," and led Clint to the back of the room.

Once he got past the bar and piano, Clint spotted a counter with a large, leather-bound book lying open on top of it. There was a pen and ink next to the book, reminding Clint of something much more like the hotel check-in he'd been expecting.

Once the man in suspenders got around the counter, Clint stepped up and placed his hands upon the polished wood surface. "I almost thought I was in the wrong place."

"Not at all, sir. The Canyon Inn caters to all your needs except for gambling and I can tell you the best places in town for that if you want. You said you needed a room?"

"That's right. My name's Clint Adams."

The man stopped and scrunched his face as though he was deep in thought. Tapping his forehead, he spun the register around and skimmed over the open page. "Ah yes. Here it is," he said while tapping a line on the page. "Miss Caudry was just here and arranged for your room. Are you a friend of hers? She was awful hard on me until I whittled down the price to her specifications."

Not wanting to get into too much detail with the talkative little fellow, Clint nodded and picked up the pen. "Where do you want me to sign?"

"Right there next to your name. Just for my records so the next shift knows your room is occupied."

Clint didn't listen too much once he saw where his name needed to go and after he'd signed, he was anxious to get off his feet for a while. The whole day seemed to be catching up to him in a rush and he nearly snatched the key from the other man's hand when it was offered to him.

"Upstairs and all the way to the back of the hall," the balding man said. "Room number twelve."

Clint tipped his hat and started walking back past the bar to where he'd seen a staircase. The hotel clerk was still talking to him, flapping his gums in what sounded like a sales pitch regarding drink specials and the like. The only part of the speech that caught his attention was that breakfast was served from six to nine in the morning.

Thankfully, the hotel was constructed so that the noise from the bar downstairs didn't make it all the way up to the rooms above. The floors were so solid that not one plank squeaked beneath Clint's feet as he made his way up to the second level and headed down the hall.

To Clint, it felt as though he'd walked about ten miles from signing the register until he got to the door marked 12. His key fit into the lock and when he turned it, there wasn't the slightest resistance from the mechanism itself. It wasn't that the lock was as well maintained as the floors, but rather it hadn't even been locked to begin with.

He made sure his gun hand was free as he opened the door and stepped inside.

The first thing he noticed was that there didn't even seem to be a bed in the room. All he could see was a coatrack, a writing desk, a sofa in front of a small fireplace, and a little table beneath a window. Just as he was about to walk back out and complain to that noisy man wearing the suspenders, Clint spotted the doorway on the wall to his left.

Taking his saddlebags off his shoulder and dropping them onto the couch, Clint moved to that doorway and looked through it. Not only was there a bed in that room, but the bed seemed to take up every available bit of space. The dim flicker of lanterns hanging from the wall on either side of the doorway gave the room a warm glow. The window was open to let in a bit of pale starlight, as well as a cool breeze.

As the wind blew in from outside, it rustled a set of expensive-looking curtains, causing the flames to flicker and the shadows to jump. But the shadows were the last things Clint was looking at. He was still taking in the sight of the large bed. Or rather, he was taking in the sight of what was waiting for him on top of that bed.

Lying on top of the soft mattress, wearing nothing but a sheet and a sultry smile, Pamela Caudry shifted luxuriously on her back as the night breeze moved over her. The cold in the air caused her nipples to stand erect beneath the sheets and she arched her back as the sensation worked its way over her skin.

"I hope you don't mind that I waited here for you," she said softly. "I was thinking I could thank you a little more for helping me out."

Clint smiled and walked over to the bedside. Looking down at her, he ran his fingers through her blonde hair and then down the side of her neck. "You've already thanked me more than enough. Don't feel obliged to do any more."

Reaching out to pull his belt open, she said, "Then how about you join me under this sheet and make love to me just for the hell of it?"

Clint let her take his belt completely off while he unbuttoned his shirt. "Well, since you put it that way . . ."

EIGHTEEN

Pamela looked up at Clint as she helped him undress. The smile on her face was similar to the one she'd been showing him the entire night, only this time there was something else that seemed to come from inside of her. He could see it in her eyes as well. There was a heat smoldering from within the blonde that made her tear his clothes off a little harder and finally pull him down onto the bed on top of her.

Bracing himself with his hands and knees, Clint dropped down until he was directly over her. He could feel her squirming beneath him until she finally tore the sheet away so she could pull him down a little closer. After the brush of cotton moved over his skin, Clint felt the warmth of Pamela's body as he lowered himself down while she arched up to meet him.

Her breasts were soft and full, their hard nipples brushing against his chest as she reached up to slide her hands behind his shoulders. Pamela's legs entwined around him as well, brushing along Clint's outer thighs in a constant flow of motion. Their bodies moved together, grinding against one another as they rolled over the entire width of the huge bed. Clint started out on top, but soon felt himself fall to one side, which allowed Pamela to mount him for a few moments. Her hair fell around them, enclosing them as if to keep the rest of the world outside.

Clint's senses were overwhelmed by her. He could smell the sweet scent of her lips and skin mixed with the fresh scent of her hair. Their hands were free to explore one another as they playfully made their way to the opposite side of the bed.

When they finally came to a stop, they were both lying on their sides, looking across into each other's eyes. Pamela opened her mouth slightly as if she was going to say something. Clint watched her and couldn't keep himself from leaning forward and kissing her deeply on the lips.

As soon as her lips touched Clint's, Pamela threw herself into the moment and hungrily returned the kiss. Her tongue darted between her lips, entwining with Clint's much the same way their legs and arms snaked around each other.

With his eyes closed and his attention fully on the touch of Pamela's lips, Clint could only feel as her hands worked down his body, touching him along the ribs while the other hand made its way between his legs. She kissed him even deeper when her hand closed around the hard shaft of his penis, stroking him up and down vigorously while the kiss grew even more passionate.

Clint's hands were busy as well. The instant he felt Pamela stroking him, he explored every curve he could find. The combination of sensations as their kiss went on when mixed with the feel of her body under his fingers made him want her even more. Her skin was smooth and hot to the touch and when he slid his hand along her plump buttocks, she opened her legs so he could caress her inner thigh.

She was moaning now as she leaned back and broke off the kiss. Every breath she took was heavy and laced with erotic groans as Clint's hand found its way to the soft, moist lips between her legs. Pamela let out a pas-

sionate cry and clenched her eyes shut when she felt Clint
gently massage the sensitive nub of her clitoris. Reflexively, she lifted one leg up and draped it over Clint's
body, opening herself completely to his touch.

Now that she was arching her head back against the
mattress, Clint could look down and enjoy the amazing
sight of Pamela's naked body. Her breasts glistened in the
dim light and her stomach moved up and down with
quickening, excited breaths. A layer of sweat was mois-
tening her skin, causing her to tremble slightly as the cool
breeze continued to work its way throughout the room.

By now, she was stroking his cock with both hands.
The wetter she got, the more she moved her hips toward
him. Even though she was aching to feel him inside of
her, Pamela didn't want Clint to stop what he was doing.
The conflict only made her more excited until she finally
reached out to grab Clint's hip and pull him closer.

"Oh god," she said. "I can't wait anymore."

Allowing himself to be guided by her hands, Clint took
hold of one of Pamela's hands and placed the other on
the sensuous curve of her backside. From there, he caressed the line along her buttocks and the top of her leg,
moving closer as she rubbed her foot over the small of
his back.

Still keeping hold of him with one hand, Pamela
moaned with anticipation as she felt his rigid penis become even more erect within her fingers. She was close
enough by then to guide him between her legs until the
tip of his cock slid into her moist vagina.

Clint could hear her start to moan with pleasure as he
entered her. Watching her face as he teased her by moving
only slightly in and out, he took firm hold of her buttocks
and thrust all the way inside, pulling her toward him as
he entered her.

Pamela dug her nails into Clint's shoulder as every one
of her muscles tensed. Her eyes shot wide open and the

noise she'd been about to make stuck in her throat as the
room became suddenly silent.

She stayed still for the next moment or two, allowing
the sensations to flow through her body. Finally, she let
out her breath and allowed a satisfied smile to crawl onto
her face. From there, she moved her hips slightly from
side to side, leaning her head back as Clint began pumping in and out of her.

Savoring every second, Clint let his hands roam over
Pamela's side as she writhed and squirmed beside him in
time to his thrusts. She moved like a cat that was reclining
and stretching in the moonlight, enjoying the feel of its
own muscles moving beneath its skin. Pamela even purred
slightly once her body found a rhythm to match Clint's
own.

She looked directly into his eyes and slid her fingers
through Clint's hair, letting out a contented breath as she
took him all the way inside of her body. Her eyes filled
with intense passion when he thrust deeply into her and
stayed in that position for a few seconds.

Savoring the moment, Clint shifted just enough to feel
his body grinding into hers. He erection was buried deep
within her moist pussy and his entire body was sur-
rounded by her skin. As far as he was concerned, the rest
of the world didn't exist. The only thing he could think
about was Pamela and the cool breeze both wrapped
around him like a blanket.

NINETEEN

Andrew Homes lifted his nose to the wind like a wolf testing for the scent of its prey. His coal-black hair was slicked down over his scalp and his thin mustache curled slightly as he allowed himself to grin. The night always felt good to the gentleman and he never missed out on an opportunity to soak it in. Even when he had so much other business to tend to, he could find time for his evening stroll.

Besides, he was fortunate enough that evening to have business that required him to walk the streets in the cool darkness. His steps thumped over the boardwalk, accompanied by the tapping of his walking stick against the wooden slats.

When he walked the streets of Estes Canyon, Homes felt that nothing could threaten him. He let his eyes wander back and forth, taking in his territory like the conquerors of old.

When he reached a particular corner, Homes stopped and planted his walking stick in front of him. He leaned on the silver handle and waited patiently, listening to the clumsy approaching footsteps with a mixture of amusement and annoyance.

After a few more seconds, Homes turned and saw two figures approaching from the shadows. They were a familiar sight to him, having been in his employ ever since he'd paid for their train ride from Cheyenne. As always, the shorter of the pair led the way, his steps somewhat wobbly after having spent a bit of time slamming drinks at a nearby saloon.

"We got here as fast as we could," Kyle said, puffing out breaths that reeked of cheap whiskey.

Homes smiled in a way that reeked of superiority. "I know you did. I could hear you both coming from half a mile away." He looked at both cowboys, one at a time. Tom was just the same as he'd left him not too long ago, so he focused in on Kyle. "Are you drunk?" he asked the shorter and more aggressive of the two.

"I been drinkin', but I ain't drunk. What of it?"

Ignoring Kyle's slurred challenge, Homes tightened his grip upon the walking stick and said, "I heard all about your run-in with this stranger that came in with Jack's horse."

Kyle looked up at the taller cowboy, balling up his meaty fists. "Who told you about it? Was it Tom here? Because he's probably just trying to cover up the way he acted on account of he about pissed himself when that stranger looked at him cross-eyed."

Rolling his eyes, Homes waved toward the shorter cowboy with a quick shooing motion. "Shut up, Kyle. You're babbling. Tom, what did you find when you went back to check up on that stranger?"

Kyle's eyes flashed with anger and he started to move toward the well-dressed Homes. "Wave at me again like that and I'll—"

Before Kyle could finish his threat, his mouth was full of cold silver, blood, and teeth. The world tilted crazily beneath his feet and he landed awkwardly on his side. His legs pumped a few times as though he was still trying to walk as he suddenly realized that he was no longer standing upright.

Kyle flipped over onto his hands and knees while his body convulsed reflexively. Not only did he kick up a bit of drunken vomit, but he puked up several teeth that had been knocked loose by the top of Homes's cane. His mouth reeking of blood and worse, Kyle dragged himself up to his feet and waited for everything to stop spinning.

Already, Homes had cocked his arm back with his walking stick resting upon one shoulder, waiting for an excuse to swing again. "What was that you were going to say?" he asked, fixing his eyes upon the furious cowboy.

After wiping the mess from his mouth with the back of his sleeve, Kyle spat out the remaining bit of bloody fluid that had collected in his throat. The drunkenness was gone completely, leaving only his anger and wounded pride. Through his shattered mouth, he said, "Nothin', Mister Homes."

The well-dressed man stared Kyle down until the shorter of the two cowboys looked away. Only then did Homes look back to Tom. "Now, as I was saying before I was so rudely interrupted, I need to know what you found out about this stranger."

"Actually, I didn't see much." No matter how hard Tom tried to keep from looking like he was afraid of the gentleman, he simply couldn't pull it off. He didn't look like he was about to run away crying, but he couldn't hold the other man's gaze either.

"All right, then. Tell me what you did see."

"I looked in on him back at Pappy's. He was sitting at a table with Pam Caudry."

Nodding slowly, Homes allowed a little smile onto his face. "Hmmm. That's interesting. Did they seem . . . close?"

"Actually, yeah. They did seem close. They were sitting together and she stayed right by him the entire time. I think she might know him from somewhere."

"Either that, or she might have just taken a shine to

him. Pamela may be sharp as a tack, but she never was the most virtuous of girls. Did you get a chance to look at the stranger's horse? Did you even think to try taking the saddlebags before he got them put away somewhere?"

Tom jumped on that one, nodding quickly. "Yes, sir, I did. I tried, but he came out before I could see much of anything. I did watch them leave together and Pam said something about getting him a room at the Canyon Inn."

Homes stepped toward the bigger cowboy, causing Tom to flinch reflexively. "You see?" Homes said while reaching out to pat the other man on the cheek. "You found out something useful after all. Not only did you find out that Miss Caudry is in good with this man, but you also know where he's staying. And if I know Pam, I'd say chances are good that he's not there alone for the night. You did good, Tom. Now go home and wait for me to get a hold of you again."

"Yes, sir, Mister Homes." And Tom headed off, more than happy to be away from the well-dressed man holding the cane.

"As for you," Homes said, pointing to Kyle. "You've still got some work to do."

TWENTY

Clint and Pamela were still lying on the bed on their sides, facing each other while moving in a slow, sensuous rhythm. Inching back slightly, Clint allowed himself to come out of her as he got to his knees and took hold of Pamela by the hips. He only had to guide her gently for her to move the way he wanted, rolling onto her stomach and getting up to her hands and knees.

Tossing her hair back and glancing over her shoulder, Pamela gave him a nasty smile and lowered her chest to the mattress, grabbed hold of a pillow and arched her back. She turned her head to one side and pressed her cheek against the soft pillow, letting out a soft moan as she felt Clint moving in behind her.

Clint ran the palms of his hands slowly over the small of her back. Pamela wiggled her hips invitingly as he caressed her backside and teased her by brushing the tip of his cock between her legs. He could feel the warmth from her vagina as he guided himself between her delicate lips. Holding her hips a little tighter, Clint pushed forward and slid easily into her wet embrace.

Feeling him move all the way inside of her, Pamela gripped her pillow tightly and let out a satisfied groan until she was completely filled. As he moved in and out of her, Clint pulled her by the hips, making every thrust feel that much more powerful.

He fell into a powerful rhythm, savoring how good she felt wrapped around him. From this angle, Clint could drive into her even deeper than before. The experience only got better when he looked down to see the glorious curve of Pamela's back and buttocks. She got herself up off the mattress and onto all fours, throwing her head back while moaning with ecstasy.

"That's it, Clint. Harder."

Clint could feel his erection become even more powerful when he heard her talk to him like that. Keeping one hand on her backside, Clint reached forward and took a hold of her hair with his other hand so he could pull her head back just until there was no slack. Even from where he was behind her, Clint could see that she was smiling widely.

"Oh my god." She groaned. "That's it. Just like that."

Pamela's breaths became faster and shallower as her body began to tense around him. She grunted every time Clint pounded into her until finally her pleasure reached its climax.

Clint thought she was going to let out a scream that would be heard all the way down the street. When Pamela lifted her head and opened her mouth, she took in a deep breath and even he could feel her body tensing for what was going to come next.

But she didn't make a sound. Instead, she let her head fall forward as her orgasm swept throughout every inch of her flesh, making her shudder as it went. Finally, she let out her breath in short bursts, groaning just loud enough for Clint to hear until finally she let her chest drop onto the mattress.

Clint could feel that he was the only thing holding her up, so he pulled out of her and let her lay down on the bed. Once again, all he needed to do was guide her with his hands and she followed his direction without question. Soon, she was lying on her back and spreading her legs for him. Clint slid inside of her and continued pumping into her while she was still reeling from her first orgasm.

The side of Pamela's face was pressed against her pillow. Her eyes were closed and she started biting the side of her index finger to keep from crying out any more. She moved along with him, grinding her hips against the base of his penis as he slid in and out of her.

Holding onto both of her legs with his hands behind her knees, Clint looked down at Pamela beneath him and felt his blood start to burn inside of him. He could feel his climax approaching and did nothing to hold it back as he continued thrusting again and again until the pleasure exploded from within him.

For a moment, he didn't want to move from his spot. The combination of what he was feeling and seeing was just too perfect for him to want it to end. Then, he felt as though his legs wouldn't support him any longer and he lay down on the huge bed next to Pamela.

"Oh my lord," she whispered after inching in close to him and draping one arm across Clint's chest. "I don't think I could move if this room caught on fire."

Laughing, Clint moved one hand through her hair. "That's funny. I felt like the room did catch fire for a second."

TWENTY-ONE

Pamela smiled and got comfortable beside him. It didn't sound like she was falling asleep, but it was plain to see that she wasn't going to be moving anywhere anytime soon.

Enjoying the flow of the cold breeze over his naked body, Clint relaxed and drank in the peaceful quiet. Since he was paying so much attention to the quiet, Clint noticed the instant it was broken.

At first, he thought it was just the sound of someone moving around outside, either in the street or possibly in the hallway. The sound came again, allowing Clint to rule out the possibility that it could have come from as far away as the street.

No, that thump he heard was too close to come from anywhere but the floor he was on. More than likely, it was coming from as close as the next room or maybe even just outside his door. He felt his heart pound inside of him when he remembered that there was a sitting room in the hotel suite and that the noise might have even come from there.

Pamela's hand flattened on his chest and she lifted her head so she could look at his face. "Clint, what's the matter? I just felt your whole body tense."

Even before she'd finished her question, Pamela saw

Clint's hand snap up and signal for her to keep quiet.

"Did you hear that?" he whispered.

Although initially annoyed by the gesture, Pamela fell silent and concentrated on any sound her ears could pick out of the dark. After a moment or two, she looked back to Clint and shook her head. "I can't hear anything, but I was also just drifting off to sl—"

Suddenly, the thump could be heard again. It sounded like something blunt being dropped on the floor or even someone accidentally bumping against a table or chair.

Pamela's body tensed as well when she heard the sound. Her arm instinctively wrapped around Clint a little tighter. "What was that?" she whispered so quietly that even Clint could barely hear her.

"I'm not sure," he answered. "But I mean to find out."

Sliding out from Pamela's embrace, Clint swung his legs over the side of the bed and cautiously pressed his feet to the floor. He didn't stand up with all his weight right away. Instead, he tested the floorboards for squeaks by easing himself down and sliding off the side of the bed. When he was off the mattress and standing in the dark, Clint had avoided making so much as a peep.

If Pamela hadn't been watching him, she might not have even known that he was off the bed at all. "Careful," she whispered.

Clint looked back and gave her a nod. When he was certain she was looking at him closely, he mouthed the words, "Stay there."

She nodded one more time before pulling the sheets up around her as though they might be able to protect her.

Making sure to keep every step slow and cautious, Clint kept his ears open and waited to hear the next time that sound broke through the silence. All the while, he worked his way toward the pile of his clothes that was laying on top of his gun belt.

Since the hotel was so well constructed, it wasn't hard

for Clint to make his way around the bed without attracting any attention to himself. In fact, the only time he had to hesitate at all was when he felt a board give slightly beneath his foot in the middle of the room. As long as he stepped where the boards came together, he didn't have any more problems.

Once he was at his clothes, he snatched up his pants and stepped into them, hopping through the legs as though he was doing some kind of jig. He didn't bother buttoning his shirt after throwing it on and immediately buckled his holster around his waist. With the weight of the modified Colt at his hip, Clint no longer felt so vulnerable to whatever it was he was after.

He checked on Pamela one more time just to make sure she was still where he'd left her. Sure enough, the blonde was huddled on the bed, watching his every move with wide eyes.

So far, Clint hadn't heard another noise since he'd made his way to his clothes. He wasn't about to let his guard down just yet, however, and started tiptoeing toward the doorway that led to the sitting room. Just as he crossed out of the bedroom, Clint heard another thump coming from somewhere just ahead. Reflexively, he backed up against the door frame and his hand flashed to the Colt's grip.

Now that he was in between the two rooms, Clint could tell that whatever was making that noise was not coming from anywhere in the suite. That was somewhat of a comfort, but not enough to get the hairs on the back of his neck to stand down.

Also, since he'd heard that sound enough times, Clint figured it was too heavy to be a footstep. If anything, it sounded like furniture being moved or something equally large being bumped against the wall.

He laughed once under his breath when he thought of the possibility that the noise was simply coming from someone in the neighboring room paying them back for the noise Clint and Pamela had been making earlier. Not everyone appreciated Pamela's groaning as much as Clint did, that was fairly safe to say. But there was something that just didn't sit right in the bottom of Clint's gut.

There was something that set his nerves to jangling and didn't let him relax until he'd figured out what the problem was for certain. That jangling had only gotten louder in the back of Clint's mind when he'd stepped into the sitting room. In fact, as he looked around and slowly took in every unfamiliar corner and each dark shadow, Clint felt his grip close around the Colt's handle.

He stopped himself before the gun came out of its holster. If he didn't have a target in his sights, he wasn't about to draw when he might just as well put a bullet into some bellhop with bad timing.

Clint was even starting to wonder if he wasn't just being overly cautious when his eyes landed on what had been causing all of his tension. There was just a little glint of light streaming in from the hallway from under the door. There was some trickling in around the edges as well, and as he'd been watching, the light around the edge of the door got brighter.

The door wasn't closed all the way. Judging by the two shadows showing beneath the door, there was someone standing in the hall at that moment, slowly pushing the door open.

TWENTY-TWO

The shadows at the bottom of the door were cast by a pair of feet.

The light on the side of the door was growing because the door itself was coming open, bit by bit.

The thumping had probably been the person on the other side of the door trying to muscle his way inside.

All of those realizations hit Clint like the proverbial ton of bricks. He only wished those bricks would have hit him a little sooner, since the door was already starting to swing inward.

In a blur of motion, Clint pulled the Colt from its holster and leveled it at where he guessed his target would be. He went reflexively for a shot that would put the other person down and as soon as the door came open, he was ready to pull the trigger.

He saw a shape moving in from the hallway, but it was coming much faster than he'd anticipated. Not only that, but it was hunkered down low so that it seemed only half as big as a normal-sized man. The moment he was certain the figure meant to rush him, Clint took his shot. Having missed his first guess cost him dearly, however, and he could tell the moment the Colt bucked in his hand that the bullet had gone over its target.

Where the room had been quiet as a grave before, it

was now full of thunderous racket. As the figure rushed toward Clint like a bull with its horns lowered, the pounding of his feet rumbled through the suite along with the roar of the pistol. Those sounds were also mixed with another. It was a harsh grunt that was a curse wrapped in a whole lot of pain.

His eyes taking in everything as though the seconds had been slowed down a notch, Clint caught a brief glimpse of the figure's face. He recognized it as the same smart-mouthed cowboy who had given him lip outside of Pamela's steakhouse.

Kyle was growling like a wounded animal as he ran forward, gritting what was left of his teeth against the pain of his newest wound. Launching himself off of the foot that was still on the ground, Kyle threw all of his weight toward Clint. He lifted his back when he'd gotten under Clint's arm in an attempt to knock the gun from his hand.

Although he was too late to take another shot at the cowboy before getting hit, Clint knew better than to let his grip around the Colt case up even in the slightest. He clenched his stomach muscles out of pure instinct less than half a second before the cowboy slammed against his solar plexus.

Even though Clint was braced for it, the smaller guy nearly took the breath right out of him. Kyle's shoulder hit Clint in the breastbone and rattled him straight down to the core. There was another impact that Clint hadn't been expecting as Kyle pressed his advantage by driving a wicked punch into Clint's gut.

Clint tried to roll with the punch as best he could, but there was only so much he could do. He allowed himself to be pushed back a step and that was so he could move one foot back to brace himself. Once that foot was firmly planted, he lifted his right hand up and pounded the Colt's handle onto the cowboy's shoulder blade.

Kyle let out another savage grunt of pain and twisted

away in case was going to take another similar shot. Straightening up to his full height, he hopped back and fixed his eyes upon Clint like an alley cat that was getting ready to pounce.

Despite the blood on his face and the snarl on his lips, Kyle somehow managed to put on the same cocky expression he'd given Clint when they were both in front of the restaurant. "You can save yourself some pain if you cooperate, fella," Kyle said as he brought his left hand up to waist level so Clint could see the small, curved blade he held. "All I want to do is ask some questions."

"All right, then. Here's your first answer." With that, Clint shifted his weight onto his front leg and swung his back leg forward with a quick burst of strength. His foot cut through the air and hooked to one side at the last second. The maneuver wasn't pretty, but it succeeded in pointing Clint's toe forward and driving the ball of his foot into Kyle's ribs.

His initial plan had been to put the toe of his boot through the cowboy's knee, but Clint had remembered that he wasn't wearing boots after he'd already launched the kick and was forced to improvise. All in all, he couldn't exactly complain since Kyle crumpled to one side and let out another pained grunt.

After everything he'd been through that evening, Kyle had developed one hell of a tolerance to pain. His mouth still hurt more than that last kick, which had mainly forced all the air from his lungs. On top of that, every move he made caused some pain from somewhere. Every bit of pain was just fueling his rage and pushing him even harder.

Clint hadn't seen the knife in the cowboy's hand until a second ago. The shorter man had charged in too fast for him to see much of anything besides Kyle's face. Now that he knew the guy had a knife, Clint was regretting the fact that he'd let him get so close.

The blade in Kyle's hand was no more than a few inches long and was curved like a fang. Not only that, but Clint thought he saw blood dripping from the wicked little blade.

He couldn't allow himself to think about that blood at the moment. If Clint let himself get too distracted, he knew he'd see plenty more of his own blood spilled upon the floor. Adjusting his body to prepare himself for the next time Kyle swung that knife at him, Clint turned sideways with the modified Colt held behind him.

"What's your next question?" Clint asked as he snapped his left hand out into a jab that just grazed Kyle's chin.

The smaller man didn't seem as groggy as Clint thought he would be and dodged a lot more of that punch than he'd expected. Kyle kept low and twisted around in a tight circle, snapping his left hand out like the end of a whip.

Clint felt a surge of adrenaline pump through him as the blade came speeding toward his stomach. He was able to keep himself from being eviscerated, but wasn't fast enough to avoid the knife completely. The tip of the blade dug in just enough to break the skin and ripped a gash across his belly that was a couple inches long.

Still moving to protect his exposed midsection, Clint twisted to bring the Colt around. But the cowboy seemed to be determined to draw blood and was already lashing out again with the knife.

TWENTY-THREE

Just as the Colt was coming to bear, Clint felt a sharp pain in his forearm. He didn't even have to look to know that he'd been torn open by that blade one more time. Although it hurt enough to draw his attention, he knew by instinct alone that the wound wasn't serious. It was probably just the cowboy's attempt to get him to drop the gun before he found himself staring down its barrel.

For that reason alone, Clint tightened his grip on the Colt and forced himself to put the pain out of his mind completely. Before he took back control of the fight, however, he decided to let the cowboy's arrogant over-confidence work for him for a change.

Clint let his gun arm drop and winced with exaggerated pain. He tried not to overplay it and noticed the smug grin on Kyle's face grow just a little bit when he saw. That smirk alone was enough to bring Clint's other hand wheeling around in a powerful arc that clipped Kyle solidly on his battered jaw.

Blood sprayed from the cowboy's mouth along with a few teeth, making Clint wonder how he could misjudge his own strength so badly. But the smaller man refused to drop and in fact followed up with a punch of his own.

Seeing that the fist headed in his direction was just that and not carrying a weapon, Clint purposely caught enough of the blow to make dropping to one knee seem realistic. Kyle didn't seem to care about realism just as long as he thought he'd done some damage.

The cowboy moved forward as blood and spit poured from the corner of his mouth. He clamped one hand around Clint's throat and pressed the blade against the side of his neck. "Now for my questions," he snarled down at Clint. "Who the hell are you and what are you doin' here?"

Clint hacked up a breath and pulled in a ragged lungful of air. "I would've told you that for free, you little pissant."

Kyle tightened his grip and pushed the blade against Clint's skin just enough to draw a few drops of blood. "Well I'm askin' you now. And if you don't tell me right quick, I'll just bury you without a name on your tombstone and be done with it."

"Clint Adams. You satisfied now? I'm here to return a horse I found."

"That a fact? You found that horse? Why come here?"

"Seemed like as good a place to start as any other. Now why don't you tell me how come you had to bust in here like this when all you wanted was to talk."

The knife bit a little more into flesh and this time Clint could hear something else along with Kyle's ragged breathing. He heard the soft patter of bare feet moving across the floor, followed by the sound of a sharp, frightened gasp.

"Oh my god, Clint, what's going on?"

"Stay back, Pamela," Clint said. "We're just here talking. Isn't that right, small-fry?"

Kyle looked down at Clint as though he simply couldn't believe what he was hearing. Even as he dragged the blade over Clint's skin, widening the shallow cut even further, his lips curled up in anger. "Shut yer mouth!

You'd better worry about keeping yourself alive instead of pissing me off."

Not moving anything but his eyes, Clint was able to see just a sliver of Pamela's leg from where he was. That was enough for him to tell if she was standing still, however, which was the only thing that really concerned him. "Don't worry, Pamela. My little pal here is about to change his tune for the better."

"Oh yeah?" Kyle said. "And how do you know so much?"

"Because you strike me as the type who prides himself on being a stallion," Clint answered as a crisp, metallic click sounded in the room, "rather than a gelding."

Although the modified Colt was a double-action pistol, Clint pulled back its hammer just for effect as he pressed the barrel up into Kyle's crotch.

When the click snapped through the air and he felt the steel jab uncomfortably into his groin, Kyle lost his smirk and every bit of cockiness that had been written upon his face. His grip around Clint's neck eased up and he pulled the knife an inch or so back.

"You know what?" Clint said as he put a few inches between himself and Kyle. "Your expression right now makes taking those punches worth every second. Of course, the fact that you hit like a little girl made it easier as well."

Clint watched the cowboy's face as his cheeks flushed and the pent-up anger began to build. "I'm not normally the cruel type," Clint said. "But I guess you just bring that out in people. Now, how about I ask *you* some questions?"

TWENTY-FOUR

Clint kept the gun right where it was as he got back to his feet and looked over to check on Pamela. She looked a little rattled as well as somewhat confused by the turn of events, but seemed to come around once she saw what was going on.

"You all right?" Clint asked her just to make sure.

She nodded and stepped back into the bedroom since she'd rushed out before putting much on to cover herself.

When Kyle started to look around at her, Clint pushed the gun in just enough to win back his attention and shook his head. "No, partner. Don't look at her. You need to worry about me and nothing else. First off, let me hear that knife hit the floor."

He'd barely finished the command before Clint heard the solid thump of the blade dropping to the ground. He felt it hit next to his boot and when he felt it with his toe, he kicked it across the room under the little writing desk.

After all he'd had to put up with from that kid, Clint was enjoying his chance to give back some grief of his own. "Good boy. Now, why don't we both get a little more comfortable and then we can talk. At the count of three, I want you to slowly go to that sofa next to you and have a seat. I'll take the steel away from your marbles, but don't forget that I can hit them just as well from anywhere in this room. Understand?"

Allowing a bit of the anger to dissipate simply because he had no other choice in the matter, Kyle nodded.

"Good. One . . . two . . . three."

The cowboy did as he was told, backing up until he all but dropped into the sofa with a grunt.

Clint could hear a group of steps in the hallway, soon followed by a familiar voice asking if everything was all right. He recognized the voice as the same one that came from the man who'd given him the room key. "Pamela, let the man outside know we've got things well in hand."

She'd already thrown on just enough clothes to be decent and padded over to the door, which was still ajar. Fielding the questions from the hotel manager that began flooding her the moment she stepped outside, Pamela still remembered to shut the door behind her.

Even though he knew she wouldn't be able to keep things in hand for too long, Clint only needed another minute or two. Of course, there was no reason to let Kyle know that. "Great. Now I can take my time and ask as many questions as I want. And if I don't like the answers, I can take my time in making you wish you were never born."

"If you're gonna shoot, than just do it," Kyle spat. "I ain't afraid of you."

"No? Well then maybe you'll be a little friendlier if we're on more even terms." With that, Clint lowered the Colt and dropped it back into his holster. "Now let's start with your name. Since you know mine, I'd say that's only fair I know yours."

"Kyle."

"Good enough. What've you got against me, Kyle? You seem to be out for my blood since I rode into this town."

Flopping back into the sofa, Kyle reached up and wiped some of the blood from his mouth.

Clint didn't wait too long before he knew he wasn't going to get anywhere with that question alone. Rather than repeat himself, he stepped up so that he was standing directly in front of the other man, but made sure to keep out of kicking distance. Staring directly into Kyle's eyes, Clint asked, "Who sent you here?"

"No one sent me."

"The only real problem you and I have is that you don't know when to shut your smart mouth and I don't mind shutting it for you. There's no reason for you to want to know why I'm in town unless you're asking for someone else, so tell me who that someone is."

Kyle looked up and met Clint's gaze. It was obvious that he meant to throw out another wise-ass comment as his reply, but stopped when he got a look at Clint's eyes. It seemed at that moment that everything that had happened fell into place. There was a time in every big talker's life when he simply couldn't avoid the fact that he was outmatched.

At that moment, the pain in his jaw wasn't fueling any fire. The aching in his ribs wasn't feeding any rage or spurring him on. Those pains just hurt and he couldn't help but flinch once Clint's hand dropped to hang over his Colt.

"Andy Homes," Kyle said. "That's who sent me. He wants to know your business here and how you know Jack MacFarlane."

"And he doesn't mind you busting in here and making a mess of this room in the process?"

"Nah. And just because you came out on top of this one, don't think he won't send more out after you the next time. It don't even matter if you kill me or not. He'll take you down." That smug little grin started to creep

back onto Kyle's face, but it went back into hiding the
moment Clint scowled disapprovingly.

"He'll get to you," Kyle said after looking away.
"Don't you worry about that."

"And that leads me right into my next question. Why
would he want to get to me so bad just because I—"

Clint stopped before finishing the question when he
heard more commotion coming from outside the suite. He
wasn't about to take his eyes away from Kyle, so Clint
asked, "What's going on out there, Pamela?"

By the sound of it, there were even more people out
there than there were just a minute ago. The footsteps had
thundered up to the door and stopped, leaving only the
voices to fill the hall. Clint recognized Pamela's and the
hotel clerk's voices, but couldn't place the deeper one that
seemed to be dominating the conversation.

Before Clint could ask again, the door opened and Pamela peeked inside. "Uh, Clint, there's a bit of a problem
here."

Suddenly, the door was pushed all the way open and
a man wearing a battered wide-brimmed hat stepped
through. What caught Clint's eye mostly was the metal
star pinned to the man's shirt.

"Clint Adams," the man announced. "You're going to
have to come with me."

TWENTY-FIVE

Pamela and the hotel clerk were both fighting for the lawman's attention as they tried to relay their own version of what had been going on. The man wearing the badge was of average build, if a little on the stocky side, and had a face covered with neatly trimmed whiskers. He barely acknowledged the two trying to talk to him as he made his way straight over to Clint.

"Looks like there's a bit of a problem here," the lawman said.

Kyle pulled himself to his feet and wiped again at the blood that was still trickling from his mouth. "I'm glad you got here, Sheriff. I think this man was about to—"

"Shut up, Kyle," the sheriff interrupted. "I don't even want to hear what you have to say since I know it'll probably just be a lie anyway. What about you, mister? You're Clint Adams, aren't you?"

"Yes, I am."

"I'm Sheriff Gellar. If you could come along with me, I'd sure appreciate it."

"Could you tell me what this is about first?"

"Actually, I was on my way over here after talking with . . ." The sheriff trailed off as he turned to level his eyes on Kyle.

The cowboy had been standing there listening to the

conversation with his arms crossed as though he was taking minutes at a city council meeting. When he saw that the lawman was staring at him, Kyle looked away.

"Get your ass moving, Kyle," Sheriff Gellar said. "And make it quick before you get yourself beaten up some more."

Spitting a juicy wad of blood and saliva onto the floor, Kyle walked toward the door and stormed into the hall. Stomping like a spoiled child, he could be heard as he went all the way through the hall and then down the stairs to the lobby.

"Before you ask, Mister Adams, I'm not really here about the scuffle you had with that one," Gellar said, hooking his thumb toward the spot that Kyle had just vacated. "I did hear some complaints about noise, but I know Kyle well enough to assume that he started it. Even if he didn't, I know he probably had it coming anyway.

"What I was about to say is that I got a visit from Ed, who owns the livery down the street a ways. That's your black Darley Arabian that was put up there tonight, wasn't it?"

"It sure is. I talked to that old man over the barrel of his shotgun this evening and he said he'd be in touch with you."

"Then I'm surprised you didn't come to see me first."

Clint could tell the lawman was testing him by throwing out questions and watching his responses carefully. He didn't mind the process one bit since there wasn't anything he particularly wanted to hide. "There seemed to be some dispute as to how I came across the other horse I brought in. I told the old man where I'd be staying if he wanted to send you after me and then I came back here to rest up. I've been riding for the last couple days and I'm tired as hell."

"No offense, Mister Adams, but you do look like hell so I've got no intention of doubting that story."

"Well, that's good to hear. By the way, I'd prefer if you call me Clint. Hearing Mister Adams all the time makes me think I'm in trouble." That was Clint's own little way of testing the sheriff, which the lawman picked up on instantly.

"That remains to be seen. But for the moment, Clint should do just fine."

"Glad to hear it."

"I've heard plenty about you, but I'll only assume half of it's true. Either way, I'm sure you know I need to take that gun from you until we get this matter straightened out."

"Please don't tell me I'll be spending the night in a cell. Not when I've got such a comfortable bed waiting for me."

"Tell you the truth, that comfortable bed of yours was the matter of one or two of the complaints when I walked in here and said I was looking for your room." The sheriff punctuated that last comment with a subtle wink before holding out his hand. "I will need that gun, though. As far as sleeping in the cell, that all depends on how our little talk goes."

Even though he didn't much like the sound of it, Clint shrugged and handed over the Colt to the sheriff. "Fair enough."

Pamela peeked into the room as though she was afraid of what she might find. "Clint, is everything going to be all right?"

"It should be fine," he answered. Looking back to Sheriff Gellar, he asked, "I want to make sure that she's protected. After all, that little shit did come busting in on us both."

"I'll have one of my deputies see that she gets home." He looked over to her and glanced her up and down. Despite the fact that he was looking at a very beautiful woman wearing nothing more than a slip that was about to fall off of her body, the sheriff kept his wits about him. "And I'll be sure it's one of the older of my bunch who gets that job. Just to be sure."

Clint grinned, even though he was being disarmed and led out of the hotel room by the town's chief lawman. "I'd appreciate that, Sheriff."

After Clint had thrown on the rest of his clothes, Gellar motioned for him to step out of the room and followed behind with his hand gripping Clint's elbow tightly. He led rather than forced Clint in the proper direction, showing respect when he could just as easily have shackled Clint in chains.

Sheriff Gellar didn't talk much on his way to his office. Not only did this apply to Clint, but to the several locals who asked him questions or tried to get some information from him as he went through the saloon and down the street. Instead, he kept his grip on Clint's gun arm and his eye on his prisoner.

Not used to being the one under the law's watchful eye, Clint still couldn't help but like the sheriff. At least the lawman was playing straight down the middle and didn't seem to be waiting for an opportunity to ambush Clint when he wasn't looking.

Of course, the night was still young.

TWENTY-SIX

The sheriff's office was a healthy walk from the Canyon Inn, but Clint didn't mind it one bit. In fact, he took advantage of the time to enjoy the quiet as well as the night air. The lawman led him around the edge of the saloon district and to a small building at the intersection of two main streets. Before either of them stepped foot on one of the stairs leading up to the boardwalk, two figures filled up the doorway in front of them.

One of the figures was a kid no more than twenty-two years old. He had the eager eyes of someone new to the job of peacemaker and tensed immediately when he saw the sheriff wasn't alone. The second man in the doorway could have filled the space by himself. His bulk was as much fat as muscle and his face was all but hidden by a full, unruly beard.

Before the kid could say a word, Sheriff Gellar pointed to him and said, "Get over to the Homes spread and check up on them, Johnny."

Surprised, the kid answered, "Yes sir, Sheriff. Should I take someone with me?"

"Just your shotgun. They're probably not looking for trouble since it looks like they had their fill already tonight. If things look like they could get rough, come back for some help. No showboating, understand?"

"Yes sir, Sheriff." With that, John marched straight down the steps and right past Clint and Sheriff Gellar.

The fat man stepped outside and was ready to follow the younger deputy anyway.

"Hold on, Bear," Gellar commanded. "Let the kid handle this one on his own. He can get help from one of the others if he needs it."

"But I don't have anything else to do, Sheriff."

"Yes, you do. I want you to go to the Canyon Inn and see Miss Caudry home. She's up in room twelve."

"See her home?"

"That's right. She's had a scare and Kyle or one of his asshole friends might be out to frighten her some more. Keep an eye on her and make sure that doesn't happen."

The deputy Gellar called Bear seemed reluctant at first to leave John on his own. When he heard what his assignment was, however, he seemed to perk up a bit.

Sheriff Gellar must have noticed that as well since he waited until Bear was down the steps before saying, "I'll tell your wife where you are. You know . . . just so she won't worry."

Bear rolled his eyes as he lumbered away from the sheriff's office. He knew damn well the only reason Gellar had mentioned his wife was to take his mind off Pamela Caudry. Clint was sure that image would be in Bear's mind even when he got a look at Pamela in the flesh.

As they walked up to the office door, Clint actually caught the lawman smirking at his put-upon deputy. It wasn't a full smile and it didn't last more than a second, but that smirk told Clint a lot about the way Gellar related to his men.

The inside of the office resembled countless other sheriff's offices that Clint had seen across the entire country. There was the rack of keys and locked gun cabinet on one wall. There were a few small desks scattered around the room with the larger, more beaten desk that surely belonged to the sheriff himself.

Just as he'd suspected, Clint was led to a chair in front of that larger desk.

There was another deputy in the office who appeared to be a few years older than the sheriff. His gray hair was thinning on top and he wore a pair of wire-rimmed spectacles that sat perched upon the end his nose like they'd been glued there.

The older deputy had been sitting at one of the desks at the back of the room when Gellar and Clint had entered and he was still there as they walked through the room. Holding a newspaper in both hands, he lowered the page he'd been reading just enough to get a look at who'd come in.

"No need to trouble yourself, Sam," the sheriff said. "Although I do have an errand for you to run."

Sam took his time folding his paper and set it down upon his desk. "This have to do with that scuffle at the Canyon Inn?"

"Nope. It's got to do with the blood coming out of Mister Adams here. Fetch the doctor and bring him back here so he can patch this man up. That is, unless you'd rather finish your reading?"

"It doesn't matter what I'd rather do," Sam grumbled.

"That's right," Gellar cut in. "Now move."

The older man didn't seem too happy about having to leave his seat, but he picked up his pace after getting a look at Clint's wounds for himself. In all the excitement, Clint hadn't worried too much about the cuts he'd gotten from Kyle's blade. They were still bleeding a bit and the dark crimson stains on his shirt already made the wounds look a whole lot worse than they were.

"Have a seat," Sheriff Gellar said while pointing to the small chair. He walked around the desk, opened a drawer, and dropped Clint's pistol into it for safe keeping. He then found a handkerchief and started cleaning the blood that had collected on his hand from where he'd taken hold of Clint's arm. "If I like what I hear, not only will you be sleeping in that big comfortable bed of yours, but you might get that weapon back as well."

"Then let's get down to it, Sheriff."

"A man after my own heart. Why don't you start by telling me what happened in that hotel room, since that's still fresh in your mind."

Although Clint left out the details of what he'd been doing right before Kyle had busted into his room, Clint told as accurate an account of the fight as he could manage. The sheriff listened with his hands folded on top of the desk, nodding every once in a while at some detail he found interesting.

When Clint was done, the sheriff asked, "So Kyle was trying to get into your room and that's how it started?"

"That's right."

"Why would he do something like that?"

"You know, I was in the middle of asking him that same thing when you came in and took over. If you or one of your men find the answer to that question, I'd sure like to hear it."

Before Gellar could respond, the door to the office opened and Sam came shuffling inside with another gray-haired man following him. "Here's the doc," Sam announced. "I pulled him outta bed so he could tend to this man just like you said."

Just going by the looks of the other man behind the deputy, Sam was telling the God's honest truth. The doctor looked every bit like a man who'd been dragged out of a deep sleep. His clothes were almost as rumpled as his hair and his shirt was only partially tucked in at odd places around his waist. In fact, even though his wounds were starting to bleed again, Clint felt a bit sorry for the poor old guy.

"You did your job, Sam, thanks so much," Sheriff Gellar said without trying to hide his sarcasm. "I'll see you get your medal. Doc, thanks for coming."

The doctor answered with a mumble followed up by a halfhearted wave. He walked over to Clint, set a black bag on the desk, and proceeded to tear the sleeve off Clint's shirt without so much as a how-do-you-do.

Once he saw that Doc was doing his part, Sheriff Gellar turned his attention back to Clint. "All right, I'll buy your story about the fight. Hell, I know Kyle well enough that nothing you said came as any big shock. Now let's get to the reason I was headed to see you in the first place."

"You want to know about Jack MacFarlane's horse?" Clint asked.

"Sure, but first I want you to tell me where Jack is and why I shouldn't think you're the reason he's missing."

TWENTY-SEVEN

Clint could tell right away that this situation was about to get messy. With Sheriff Gellar looking at him with intense scrutiny, Clint knew that the way he answered this next question could mean the difference between walking out of the office or spending some time in a cell. Since his instincts had served him pretty well this far, Clint decided to let them guide him a little bit more.

Slowly, Clint reached for the photographs that were still folded in his pocket. He flipped to the one with the man and both women and set it on the desk. "Is that Jack MacFarlane?"

Gellar reached out, spun the pictures around so he could see them right-side up, and studied the frozen image for a second. "Yep. That's him, Bonnie, and Luanne. Where'd you get these pictures?"

"I found them on Jack's body. His body was tied to his horse and when I found them, that horse was running as though the devil himself was chasing it."

Once again, the sheriff looked up at Clint so he could study the other man's eyes. His face was a stony mask and the expression he wore hadn't shifted one bit after hearing the bad news regarding Jack. After taking a moment to soak it in, he placed his hand flat upon the stack of pictures and said, "The first thing a man learns when he puts on a badge is that the most obvious answer is usually the right one. Whoever's holding the smoking pistol usually pulled the trigger."

"I could have just as easily let that horse keep running," Clint said in his own defense. "I came back because he was murdered and it looked like he had unfinished business with someone here in town."

"One of these ladies?" Gellar asked, tapping the photograph on top of the stack.

Clint nodded. "It just didn't seem right to let a man be treated like that, even if he was dead."

"I can understand that well enough."

"Look, Sheriff, I'm sure you know who I am." Normally, Clint didn't like trading on the dubious value of his name or reputation. In fact, more often than not, he found it a damned nuisance to have to deal with folks who thought they knew him just because they'd read a few yellowback novels. But this was one of the rare times he took the gamble and tried to make that reputation work for him for a change.

Gellar nodded. "I've heard the name before."

"Then you might also be able to understand that I'm not the type of man to kill someone and steal his horse. Something tells me you already figured I wasn't that type, which is why I'm sitting at this desk instead of behind bars right now."

Reading the sheriff just as much as he was being read himself, Clint looked Gellar in the eyes as he spoke. So far, he could tell the lawman was open to what he was hearing as well as ready to change his mind at a moment's notice.

"I came back because of this," Clint said while removing the folded letter from his inside pocket. "Also, after all that I've been through since I stepped foot in this town, I've taken a personal interest in what happened to this Mister MacFarlane. You can accept my word and let me work with you or you can lock me up. It's your decision."

Finally, Sheriff Gellar leaned back in his chair and rubbed the stubble on his chin. He took a few deep breaths and clenched his jaw as though he was literally chewing on what he'd just heard from Clint. Before too long, he reached out and pushed the stack of photographs back across the desk. "I have heard of you, Mister Adams. The trick is that a lot of men are jealous of a reputation like yours and decide it's easier to walk around saying they're the Gunsmith rather than earn a reputation of their own."

"Sheriff, I can assure you that I'm not—"

Cutting Clint off with a sharply raised hand, Gellar leaned forward and opened his desk drawer. "A friend of mine's a U.S. Marshal and he met you about three years ago. I doubt you remember him, but he sure as hell remembered you. He said you were a stand-up fella and lived up to all the good things he'd heard about you.

"But more than your face or your horse, he remembered something else even more vividly." With that, the lawman took out Clint's holstered gun and set it carefully on the desk. He drew the weapon and held it on its side in both hands. "More than anything else, he remembered your gun. Specially crafted, custom-modified double-action Colt," Gellar recited while looking down at the weapon in his hands. "That friend of mine talked about this gun like it was the love of his life and he kept talking about it until I swear I was about to fall in love with it myself. Since the death of Clint Adams would have been news that I'd have heard by now, I'm inclined to believe you are who you claim to be."

After taking one last look at the Colt, Sheriff Gellar holstered it and pushed it across to Clint. "That's one hell of a fine piece of craftsmanship, Mister Adams."

"Thanks for noticing," Clint said earnestly. "What else did this U.S. Marshal friend of yours say about me?"

"He said you were the type to avoid killing a man until

there was no other option left to you. So you might say that keeping Kyle alive also played a part in my decision to keep you out of jail."

Clint stood up and buckled his holster back around his waist where it belonged. "I'll be sure to thank him the next time he's trying to cut a piece out of my hide."

"Well, knowing Kyle the way I do, you probably won't have to wait too long for that to happen. That's why I'd prefer to know you're working on my side on this."

"So would I, Sheriff."

"Good. Now I heard some of the story from Ed, but let's hear it all from you, starting with the moment you found that horse."

The very thought of having to go through all of that story one more time was nearly enough to make Clint want to pull his hair out by the roots. But even that was a hell of a lot better than trying to get the sheriff's attention from the inside of a jail cell.

Reluctantly, Clint started in on what had happened.

TWENTY-EIGHT

"All right. So what happened after that?"

Kyle took another swig from his bottle of cheap whiskey and gritted his teeth as the alcohol burned down his throat after tearing through the ravaged, broken innards of his mouth. "After that, the sheriff let me go and I went."

Andrew Homes had been listening to the words coming out of the cowboy's mouth for what felt like an entire week. As he spoke, Kyle kept drinking more whiskey and his voice became more slurred and garbled. It was all Homes could do to keep from hitting the smaller man, but that was only because he knew doing so would only make Kyle's speech worse.

"And that's it?" the well-dressed man asked. "You just left it at that?"

"What the hell else did you want me to do? I already got my face kicked in and nearly got my dick blown off by that crazy son of a bitch. You want me to get myself killed while I'm at it?"

Without batting an eye, Homes replied, "That would have at least saved me the trouble of doing it myself."

For a second, Kyle stared at the other man with his face frozen in a slack-jawed expression. Suddenly, he spat out a couple rough laughs and took another pull from the whiskey bottle. "Yeah, right. Sometimes I don't know when you're kidding."

"So you didn't really learn too much while you were there," Homes stated. He knew he would have to draw anything useful out of the cowboy since Kyle had been drinking. Not only did that fact annoy him, but it made his hand clench a little tighter around the top of his walking stick. "And since that was why you were there, it's safe to say that you didn't do what I sent you there to do."

"Oh, I got some information you wanted, but I don't know how good it is. That stranger said his name was Clint Adams."

"I've already heard that much. Go on."

Kyle had to pause for a second to pull the rest of what he was going to say out of his pickled brain. After a rank burp gurgled up from his gullet, the cowboy said, "He said he was in town to return a horse."

"That's all?"

"Yeah. That's all."

Whether or not there was more to be said, Homes could tell that he wasn't going to get much more out of the smaller man besides foul breath. Besides, he'd heard more than enough to satisfy him for the moment. "All right. You've done good enough, I suppose. Now get the hell out of here before you stink up the place more than you already have."

Kyle was more than happy to oblige, but he was having trouble getting up from his chair. He flopped from side to side like a turtle that had been flipped onto its back.

Reaching out a hand in the cowboy's direction, Homes leaned forward and smacked the walking stick against the arm of the chair less than an inch from Kyle's wrist. That brought the other man reflexively to his feet where he swayed as though he was about to keel over at any second.

"Did you see anything else at all before you went and bought that alcohol using my money?" Homes asked.

"The sheriff took the stranger away and a couple minutes after that, that fat-ass deputy of his came by to walk that whore back home. That's it."

The last couple words of Kyle's report barely made it through the door as he shut it behind him on his way out. Homes could still hear the drunken cowboy prattling on to himself as he staggered away. Just to make sure he didn't get any more visitors during the night, Homes went over to the door and locked it.

Only when he could no longer hear the slightest trace of Kyle's voice did he allow himself to truly relax. Being the biggest house on the entire spread, Homes had his pick of rooms when he put the front door behind him and started working his way back through the building. He settled on the study, where he conducted most of his business and set himself down on the edge of a large mahogany desk.

After carefully placing the walking stick against a nearby chair, he pressed the tips of his fingers against his temples and let out a controlled breath. Ever since this business with Jack MacFarlane had started, Homes hadn't gotten a good night's sleep that lasted more than two hours. His mind was constantly bogged down by that man's face, even though he knew for certain that Jack's eyes would never open again.

He thought he'd buy himself some peace by tearing Jack apart and driving him out of town, but the dead man was still with him, tormenting him from the grave. He could still see MacFarlane laughing at him. That laughter was even loud enough to drown out the screams that had come from his mouth just before he'd passed on.

As much as Homes wanted to help himself to one of the expensive bottles of Scotch lining the back of the room, he knew he couldn't do that until this matter was truly put to bed once and for all. If he needed more reason not to toss back a drink or two, all he needed to do was think about Kyle making an ass out of himself. After that, a glass of water sounded just fine.

"Jesus Christ." He groaned when he thought about the name that belonged to the stranger who had just arrived in town.

In fact, Homes didn't have any doubt that that man was indeed Clint Adams. The way things had been going, having the Gunsmith after him was the only way things could go bad. He'd thought he had everything tied up so nice and neat. It would have taken something big to knock Homes back down to where he'd started.

Out of force of habit, he reached over to a picture frame that was standing on top of the desk. The carved wood was so familiar in his hands that there were dark stains in the varnish that were the exact shape of his fingers.

Homes gazed down at the picture and felt the rage build up inside of him until he thought he was right back in the dark place he'd been the last time he'd seen Jack MacFarlane alive. The heat in his stomach was so intense that it burned up to his chest and made his blood boil within his veins.

That was what he'd needed. That rage serviced him ten times better than any amount of alcohol he could consume. The more he stared down at that framed picture, the more powerful he felt until finally he caught himself thinking that he might be ready to face down the Gunsmith without any help at all.

That was how he'd felt when he'd watched MacFarlane die. Homes savored that memory the same way he'd used to savor looking at the picture in his hands. Now, that memory as well as that picture were just matches dropped onto the kerosene in the pit of his stomach.

Without knowing it, Homes was clenching his hands

around the frame until the pieces of wood started to strain against the nails holding them together. He stopped himself before breaking the frame apart and let out the breath he'd been holding.

For a moment, the storm within him seemed to pass. Suddenly, in a burst of pent-up energy, Homes whipped his hand to one side and sent the frame sailing across the room. It turned once through the air before impacting against the wall and shattering into broken glass and splinters.

Homes merely watched; his anger spent and his energy gone. From the other side of the room, Luanne Parkinson's frozen smile looked back at him from the picture, which now sat amid the remnants of its frame. Homes wanted to leave, but he just couldn't get himself to look away.

TWENTY-NINE

"So now that I've filled you in," Clint said after he was done relaying his account to the sheriff, "do you think you could fill me in on a thing or two?" He'd told the lawman everything that had happened except for the fate of Jack MacFarlane's tongue.

Before Sheriff Gellar could answer, the doctor who had been working on Clint's arm straightened up and rubbed the side of his neck. He'd been working so quickly and so expertly that both Clint and the sheriff had nearly forgotten he was there.

"That about does it," Doc said. "If you break them stitches, come by to see me. I'll send my bill here and you two can fight over it in the morning. I need to get some sleep."

Waiting for Doc to leave, the lawman rubbed his eyes and shrugged. "I'll answer what I can, but I think we'd both do better after taking Doc's advice for ourselves. We both could use some sleep."

"Well, I'd sleep better knowing if I should keep one eye open or not."

For the first time since they'd met, Sheriff Gellar allowed himself to act like someone who didn't have the power to lock Clint up at any given second. When he stood up and stretched his back, the lawman yawned and said, "I'm not gonna lie to you. You might want to be on your guard if you still want to stay in town. Mister Homes may not run this place, but he does have a lot of people working for him who think he does. And since that was one of his boys that came after you, I'd lay good money that there'll be more on your tail."

"For what? Not letting that little rat push me around outside a restaurant?"

"Nope. For bringing back something that Mister Homes probably thought he'd never see again."

"Just who is that guy, anyway?"

"Andy Homes came here with a lot of money from back East and started up a ranch outside of town. It's an impressive spread and it's made him even more money over the years. Homes is the type of man who thinks he can buy just about anything or anyone that he wants. That kind of thinking didn't make him too popular around here, especially with them who got a thrill from telling him no."

"You mean Jack MacFarlane?"

Gellar looked at Clint and nodded. "Him and some others. But Jack got an extra thrill from having something a rich man couldn't get. It started out with a piece of land across the river from Homes's ranch. Once he knew he couldn't get his hooks into that, Mister Homes started hassling Jack any chance he got.

"There were a few harsh words and then a few fist-fights between Jack and some of Homes's boys. After one of them drew blood, it started getting personal."

Clint had gotten to his feet as well. Pulling on his jacket, he winced as his freshly stitched wounds flared up just to let him know he'd stretched a bit too much in the wrong direction. The pain actually did Clint a favor by waking him up like a splash of cold water on his face. "Just how personal did it get?"

"Jack never had much," Gellar said. "He's a lot like most folks and so he didn't have hardly anything that a richer man could buy or steal away from him. And what he did have, Jack guarded like a dog with a bone in its mouth.

"What little things Jack owned started turning up missing. I'd hear about that when some livestock was stolen in the night or a wagon wheel was busted by some punk kids who just so happened to do odd jobs for Mister Homes. Before too long, the fights between Jack and the rest started getting bloody. Soon after, folks who called themselves friends of Jack MacFarlane started getting hurt as well and for no better reason than sticking their heads out when the likes of Kyle or Tom walked by."

"And what did you do about that?" Clint asked.

"I did my damn job, thank you very much! I tossed Kyle and them others into my jail more times than I can count. Even tossed ol' Jack in there as well. But there's only so much I could do when both parties that're fighting decide to keep the matter between themselves."

Clint walked next to the sheriff as he headed for the front door. Besides the old man still reading his paper, there was another deputy about to come on duty who stepped inside just as Clint and Gellar were about to leave.

"That sounds a lot like a good old-fashioned feud," Clint said.

Sheriff Gellar chuckled and stepped aside so the deputy could get by. "That's right. And any man who's been anywhere near a feud knows it's healthiest to keep the hell away from it. Far away."

"Is that your advice for me? Stay far away from this whole thing?"

"Hell no, Adams. With a man like you around, I figure I might be able to get this damn thing settled once and for all."

"I thought that having Jack turn up dead would have pretty much ended the feud right there."

"The feud, yes. But feud or no, I don't take kindly to

men killing folks in my jurisdiction. I thought that Jack might have been keeping himself hid for a while until some of this blew over. But if he's dead—"

"Oh, he's dead, Sheriff," Clint interrupted. "I can even tell you where the body is if you'd like to check on it yourself."

"I'd like to take you up on that offer. It's not that I don't trust you, but Jack deserves a decent burial, even if he did bring some of this on himself."

"No problem."

"And since he's dead," the sheriff said, picking up from where he'd left off, "I want to make sure Mister Homes pays for it. I don't care how rich he is, he doesn't got some kind of hunting license in this town. Now, since I took you to your word and treated you like a gentlemen, Mister Adams, I was hoping you'd be up to returning the favor."

Clint was starting to feel a little uneasy when he heard that. "All right. Are you looking for another deputy?"

"No, no. Quite the opposite, in fact. I was hoping I'd have someone I could count on working for me without him being marked by wearing a star on his chest."

"Sheriff, I like the way you think."

THIRTY

Clint had been thinking about another one of Mister Homes's gunmen paying him a visit sometime during the night. After seeing the first one in action, he wasn't so worried about getting taken out by another clumsy ambush as he was concerned that one of them would be cowardly enough to try and finish him off when he was asleep.

But Clint had never been the type to let anyone rattle him, especially the bullying kind. What it all came down to, however, was that big comfortable bed. All Clint had to do was get near it and he all but fell onto the mattress and drifted instantly to sleep.

He trusted his instincts well enough to wake him if anyone came around to kill him.

The next morning, Clint woke a few hours after dawn. It was a little later than his normal time, but that wasn't too surprising considering all he'd been through the day before. His room was quiet as when he'd slept outside without a town around him for miles in every direction, thanks to the sturdy floors and walls. Shuddering to think about what the regular nightly rate for that suite was before Pamela's discount, Clint pulled on his clothes and headed downstairs for breakfast.

With Pamela still on his mind, Clint made it to the stairs before the scent of sausage, ham, eggs and potatoes hit his nostrils. He hurried the rest of the way down the stairs and stopped at the bottom once he realized he didn't know exactly where the dining room was.

To his right, he could see a few people scattered around the bar, but his nose told him to go right and when he turned that way he found himself heading toward a doorway at the end of a short hall. Pulling in so many tasty smells with every breath, Clint could practically taste his breakfast before even entering the large room filled with tables and chairs.

There were several small groups of people waiting to be seated, making Clint regret not having gotten out of bed just a little earlier. Before he could get too cranky, however, he saw a familiar face smiling at him from a table halfway across the room.

"Excuse me," he said to a young man with a pad and pencil in hand. "I think I've already got a seat waiting for me."

He walked through the room, dodging chairs as they were scooted out in front of him and waiters who sped around with trays full of food and glasses. When he finally made it to the right table, he had to brace himself as Pamela came rushing toward him to place a warm kiss on his lips.

"I was hoping you'd come down soon," she said happily. "I'm so glad you're not in jail!"

Clint looked around at all the faces that turned to look at him upon hearing that strange introduction. "Yeah. Me, too. How about we sit down so I can get so I can get some food into me?"

"Oh sure," Pamela said with an apologetic shrug. "It's just that I thought you might be in trouble after what happened. I heard that Ed didn't paint too good of a picture of you when he called in the law."

"If you're talking about that old man at the livery stable, then you're absolutely right. He didn't make me look too good at all. Somehow I managed to dig myself out of that hole."

"That's wonderful."

"But then I got myself right into another one."

Although Pamela put on a frown, it was plain to see that she was only doing a poor job of hiding the fact that she was still very glad to see him. And rather than try to dampen her spirits, Clint took hold of her hand to give it a loving squeeze.

"Thanks for getting this table," he said. "Not having to wait in that line is a good start to the day. I thought I'd have to start some trouble if I didn't get some of that food I'd been smelling into me real quick."

Either the staff at the restaurant was extremely good, or Pamela had made the waiter wait for Clint to arrive. Clint guess it was the latter since the waiter talked to them as though he just couldn't get his words out fast enough. Pamela ordered pancakes and bacon and Clint ordered just about one of everything with some coffee to wash it down. The waiter scribbled on his pad of paper and jogged away.

"I would have stayed the night with you," Pamela said after leaning in close enough to speak privately, "but a deputy came by and practically dragged me home."

"I hope you mean *your* home."

"Well, I don't know how much safer he thought I'd be sleeping there or in your room since everyone in town knows who I am anyway. Mister Homes knows, so that's all that matters. I swear I thought he only had a problem with poor Jack. I didn't think he'd try anything like what happened last night with someone who's not even a part of anything."

"So how much do you know about all of this?" Clint asked. Before he got a re-telling of the story Sheriff Gellar had spun the other night, Clint clarified his request a little bit. "Who's this Bonnie Shaughnessey and Luanne Parkinson?"

With her smile turning sour at the mention of those names, Pamela shrugged and said, "Maybe I should have invited them to breakfast with us."

"I know you don't think too much of Luanne, but do you think you could see your way clear to an introduction at least?"

After giving him a stare that could have frozen the water in every glass in the restaurant, Pamela finally said, "Fine. I can introduce you. She's probably too wrapped up in herself to remember why I wouldn't want to see her anyway."

Clint was a little curious about that himself, but rather than keep the subject open any longer than was necessary, he let it drop with a simple, "Thanks for that, Pamela."

She was just as glad to stop talking about it as he was, and soon the smile was coming back onto her face.

THIRTY-ONE

The breakfast was every bit as good as Pamela had built it up to be the night before. By the time it was served, Clint was ready to tear into the field of plates that were set in front of him. Of course, he was hungry enough to have eaten a napkin by mistake without noticing.

Pamela watched with an amused look on her face and picked at her own meal, which looked like a children's helping in comparison. The coffee was flavored with nutmeg, which Clint didn't pick up on until he forced himself to slow down a bit.

"Good lord," Pamela said. "I hope you remember to come up for air sometime soon."

Grinning while wiping at his face with a napkin, Clint finished what was in his mouth and put his fork down. "I could take a breather, I suppose."

"Are you finally stuffed to the top of your eyeballs?"

"No, I said I could take a breather. Tell me, are you going to be upset if I ask a question about Bonnie Shaughnessey?"

"No. Not at all. Bonnie is a sweetheart and I am so glad you got that letter for her. I mean, after what happened to Jack and everything, she deserves to read his last . . ." Although she didn't look ready to cry, Pamela clearly was uncomfortable with the thought of what had really brought Clint to Estes Canyon.

"So they had a good relationship?" Clint asked once he was fairly certain Pamela didn't want to finish what she'd been saying.

She nodded. "I'm not her best friend or anything, but I know her well enough to know how she felt about Jack. They were trying to keep things secret, but they both met in my restaurant quite a bit and I got to talking to her one time when he didn't show up until late."

"Secret? Is Bonnie married to someone else? Come to think of it, was Jack married?" Suddenly, Clint was struck by the fact of how little he really knew about Jack MacFarlane. It seemed strange considering how much he'd gone through for the dead man.

"No, it's nothing like that. But Jack wasn't exactly a healthy man to know once he started tangling with Mister Homes. Friends of Jack's started getting hassled here and there, so he wanted to keep it under his hat how close he and Bonnie had gotten."

"Well that goes along with what the sheriff was telling me last night. Actually, I'd say it was pretty smart for a man in Jack's position."

"What position?"

"Of being the target of a rich man with a grudge. That's not a good place to be. Believe me," he said, thinking back to plenty of other instances in his own life where he'd wound up in some man's crosshairs, "I know what I'm talking about on that one."

After thinking about it for a few seconds, Pamela shivered as though she'd caught a chill and took a sip of her nutmeg coffee. "Well, I don't like the thought of being hunted by someone like that. Jack only told me a little bit about it so I would know to keep quiet if anyone asked around my place, but that was enough to scare me for weeks. Especially when you see the things Mister Homes has done."

"Anyone ever get hurt too badly?" Clint asked, trying to keep his tone casual so as not to alarm Pamela any more.

"There were a lot of fights and always some scuffle in a saloon whenever Jack and his friends got around too many boys from the Homes spread."

"Any shooting?"

"Not really. At least, not as far as I know. I try not to think about it unless I have to." She took a bite of toast and shrugged. "Looks like now I have to, though."

"Yeah, well, you don't have to think about it too much. This still isn't your problem. Just because you're around me I don't want you to get pulled into this thing. I already feel bad enough about what happened last night."

"Really? Because I've been thinking about last night and I wouldn't mind doing that again real soon."

"Not *that*," Clint said. "You know what I mean."

"Yes, I know. And don't feel bad. That had nothing to do with you."

"Then it's settled. We move on and after breakfast you take me to meet Bonnie Shaughnessey."

Pamela leaned in a bit and said, "What about the good part of last night? I'm still thinking about it."

"Oh yeah," Clint said as he started tearing into the rest of his food. "We'll be doing that again real soon."

THIRTY-TWO

When Pamela led Clint out of the Canyon Inn, he felt so full he could barely walk at a regular pace. Once he got his feet moving and some fresh air in his system, his steps came a lot easier and he could feel the exercise working for his digestion.

"Come on, slowpoke," Pamela said as she pulled his hand like an impatient little girl.

"Give me a break here. I feel like I'm carrying around about ten extra pounds."

"Well that'll teach you not to stuff yourself like that the moment you roll out of bed." Circling around to the other side of him, she took hold of his hand and walked so that her shoulder was rubbing up against his. "I know a good way we can work that off later. Or even now."

Clint couldn't help but be tempted by the offer, but he knew better than to tell her that. "Business first, then we can take it from there."

She showed him an exaggerated pout and lowered her eyes. "You don't want to anymore?"

"It's not that, but I just—" Clint already saw the smirk on her face and knew that she wasn't even close to being seriously upset with him. "It's just that I think you might hurt me because you get so rough. Maybe I'm not used to sharing my bed with women like that."

126

"What did you say?" Pamela stopped and snatched her hand away. "I cannot believe you would—" This time, she was the one who stopped when she saw that Clint was now teasing her. She took his hand again and resumed walking. "Kid around all you like. We'll see who's begging who when all is said and done."

"That's no mystery. If all it takes is a little crawling at your feet, I'll be there. Besides, I might think of some things to do while I'm down there that you might like."

Pamela turned her head and lifted her free hand to cover her growing smile.

"Are you blushing?" Clint asked with genuine amazement. "I do believe you are!"

"Believe what you want," she said from behind her hand. "Just try to control yourself while we're here. This is Bonnie's place."

They'd walked a couple streets over from the hotel to a row of shops and small houses built fairly close together. The area looked as though it had probably started out on the outskirts of town, but was integrated into the rest once Estes Canyon expanded a bit. The spaces between the buildings was uneven, but not nearly as cramped as the alleys found between the saloons and shops in the business district. All in all, it was a quiet area within walking distance of open trail.

Clint stopped in front of the little home Pamela had pointed to and lifted her chin with his finger. After seeing that there was indeed a bit of extra color on her cheeks, he leaned down and kissed her gently. "I really appreciate all this help, Pamela."

"I know. Now let me introduce you first." With that, she walked up the two steps leading to a front porch that wasn't much bigger than the table where they'd eaten breakfast. She knocked on the door and shifted her eyes to the edge of the closest window, which was covered with clean, white lace curtains.

In a matter of seconds, Clint could hear footsteps coming from inside the house and then the curtains were pulled aside, allowing a face to peek out in the space where Pamela was already looking. Pamela smiled, waved, and stepped back as the face disappeared from the window.

Clint could hear the latch being moved and then the door swung open to reveal the woman, whom he recognized from the pictures in Jack MacFarlane's pocket.

"Good morning," Pamela said in a friendly, sympathetic voice. "Do you mind if we come in for a bit?"

"Who's that?" the redhead asked, looking past Pamela to Clint.

Pamela stepped aside and said, "This is Clint Adams. Clint Adams, this is Bonnie Shaughnessey."

Clint removed his hat and held out a hand in greeting. "Nice to meet you, ma'am."

Although Bonnie didn't seem offended that Clint was there, she didn't shake his hand either. Clint didn't really expect a warm reception. That would have only made it harder for him to break the bad news to her. As it was, Bonnie seemed ready for the worst.

Pamela was obviously getting uncomfortable with the way things were starting off. "Do you mind if we come in?" she asked again. "It's really important."

Bonnie nodded and held the door open as she stepped to one side. Pamela walked into the little house with Clint following right behind her.

The house was neat and orderly, but seemed unusually still. Although he wasn't much of a believer in spirits or anything like that, Clint knew there were certain emanations that houses gave off. Houses simply felt different if they were occupied by an elderly widow as opposed to a family with five kids. Whether those kids were home or not, the house kept a bit of them like pictures on a mantle.

Bonnie's house was full of the usual furnishings and

even smelled like she'd just finished breakfast herself. But despite all of that, the place still felt deserted. In fact, it almost felt as though they were borrowing a house from people who'd moved on a long time ago.

The air itself had a stillness that felt like the cool breeze on Clint's skin. The only difference was that he didn't find that particular cool breeze all that comforting.

After shutting the door, Bonnie stood with her hands folded in front of her and looked first at Clint and then to Pamela.

For a moment, it seemed as though both Pamela and Clint were too affected by the cool stillness to move. They all looked at each other for a few awkward moments before Pamela finally shattered the quiet.

"We won't be long," she said. "If we're interrupting something, I apologize, but—"

When Bonnie spoke, her meek voice cut right through everything else. "Jack's dead, isn't he?"

This was the part Clint had been dreading.

THIRTY-THREE

Rather than try to come up with something to say at that moment, Clint lowered his eyes respectfully and forced himself to nod in response to Bonnie's question.

"He had this," Clint said, doing his best to pay close attention to the words he used before they came out of his mouth. He removed the sealed letter and held it out toward the redhead. "It was in his pocket and I think he meant to deliver it to you."

Bonnie stared at Clint as though she hadn't heard him. But before he repeated himself, she reached for the letter Clint was offering and grasped it in both hands. After looking down at the writing with her name and address on the front, she pressed the letter against her breast and closed her eyes tightly.

"I was afraid this day would come," she said. "After not hearing from him for so long, I just knew something bad had happened to Jack. I just knew it."

"How long has it been?" Clint asked.

"Almost two weeks since I last saw him. He's been around here and there, but he couldn't come to see me. It was too dangerous, he said. I knew that, but he's never been gone this long. I was afraid that . . ." Tears formed at the corners of her eyes and she swallowed hard to choke them back. She only had to reach up and dab one away that dripped down her cheek before she could control it. "I guess I was right to be afraid."

Pamela went right over to her and wrapped both arms around Bonnie's shoulders. "You poor thing. I'm so sorry any of this had to happen to you or Jack. I'm sorry it had to happen at all."

Bonnie nodded and took a few deep breaths. By the time Pamela let go of her, she seemed to have moved a few steps back from the verge of crying. "Why don't we sit down," she said in a shaky monotone. "I think I'll need to sit down before I read this."

Clint followed the two women as they led him to a small sitting area about ten feet away from the front door. There was a small sofa that had seen better days in between a set of matching chairs, which were all positioned around a chipped coffee table. The coffee table was bare except for a cup that looked as though it had been emptied several days ago and left there to dry. That single cup made Clint think again about how deserted the house felt.

Bonnie looked at the letter and reread the front. Moving her fingers beneath the folded side, she broke the seal with a quick motion that sent bits of wax to the floor and tabletop in front of her. She didn't move right after that. Instead, she kept the letter closed between her thumb and forefinger.

"Do either of you want something to drink?" she asked, looking up suddenly from the piece of paper in her hands.

Clint shook his head. "No. Don't worry about us. We're both—"

"Parched," Pamela cut in. "We were just talking on the way over how nice a tall glass of lemonade would taste. I think Clint thought you were talking about alcohol."

Although Clint was a bit taken aback by Pamela's quick interruption, he could tell she wanted him to get up just like she was doing. He followed her lead and found himself being all but dragged away as Pamela took off down the short hall leading to the back of the house.

"I'll take care of him, Bonnie," Pamela said without breaking stride. "I know where everything is."

Before he knew it, Clint was swept out of the front room and found himself in a cramped little kitchen that was filled mostly by a cupboard, a pantry, and a potbellied stove. He figured Bonnie must have spent most of her time in the kitchen since that was the first room that felt truly alive in the entire house.

Pamela had let go of his hand and was flitting around the kitchen, gathering up a pair of glasses and a pitcher of lemonade. "Sorry about that, Clint," she said in a soft voice. "But I just knew she wasn't about to open that letter with both of us in there watching her. I thought I'd give her some time alone so she could do it in private."

Clint felt bad simply because he hadn't thought of that himself. "It's all right. Actually, some lemonade does sound pretty good."

After filling both glasses, Pamela put the pitcher back where she'd found it and took a sip of the sour, yellow liquid. "What do you think it says?" she asked once Clint had drained half of his own glass.

"I don't know. I didn't read it."

"You didn't even peek?"

"Nope."

She shook her head and took another sip. "I don't know if I could've helped myself. You must be a saint."

Clint laughed and shook his head. "I've been called plenty of things, but that's really too high on the list."

"I'm serious. Any other man I know would have taken that horse and everything else he could find and then sold it a few towns away. After all, it's not like anyone was going to claim it."

"So I'm not a thief or a grave robber. That's still a long way from sainthood."

After setting down her glass, Pamela stepped up to

Clint and stood directly in front of him. She had to get on her tiptoes to look directly into his eyes, but she did that and held his gaze for a few seconds. "You're a good man. Take your compliments when you can get them."

Although he wasn't a big one for savoring compliments, Clint did think of something else he wanted to enjoy while he had a chance and he took that moment as his chance. Pamela seemed a little surprised when he moved his head forward just enough to press his mouth against her lips. The first kiss was quick and gentle, but the one after that was longer and more passionate.

Pulling away before too long, Pamela ran her hands up and down Clint's arms. "I should go back in there and check on Bonnie." She walked out of the kitchen, taking a deep breath to prepare her for whatever she might find.

THIRTY-FOUR

"Lovely day," Andrew Homes said as he tipped his bowler hat to the closest lady that could hear his voice. Homes had walked those same streets for the last several years and seen many of the same faces every day, but didn't care enough to remember their names.

Recoiling a bit at first, the older lady clutched her handbag a little tighter and then plastered on a smile in return. "It certainly is, Mister Homes."

Homes nodded once more and then continued his stride, leading every step with his expensive silver-tipped walking stick. Another pair of younger women strolled by on his left and he tipped his hat to them as well. "Good morning, ladies."

Those two merely nodded and went about their business.

Judging by the smile on his face, one might have thought that Homes had gotten a kiss on both cheeks from all three of those women in exchange for his chipper words. The truth of the matter was that he barely remembered them, but that was no different than any other day. What was different was the path that Homes took as he made his way down the street and turned his back to the gambling and saloon district.

He would normally start his day with a stiff drink and

check in with his men, but this was no ordinary day. Rather than walk through the same doors as usual, he kept his pace brisk and his feet moving while whistling a happy song.

The night before hadn't been a complete success, but enough had gone right for Homes to be happy about. He knew who he was dealing with and the sheriff was taking steps to keep an eye on Clint Adams, which meant that Homes didn't have to waste time doing that job himself. And with the law keeping Adams busy, it would only be a matter of time before Homes could return to business as usual.

He knew there was a lot more that needed to be done before the entire affair could be put to rest, but things were moving along nicely. At least, that's the way he figured it after thinking it over during his breakfast of biscuits and gravy.

Everything always looked better on a full stomach. Everything looked even better than that when Homes knew he was going to pay a visit to one of his favorite places in town. With all that had been going on, he simply couldn't get that familiar, beautiful face out of his mind. The instant he decided to pay her a visit so he could see that face in person, maybe even reach out and touch it, he knew he was doing the right thing.

There was risk, sure.

There were things that could go wrong, as always.

But the warmth he felt inside made Homes think that every bit of risk was well worth it. He knew he could only feel better once he got to where he was going and set his eyes on the object he'd been coveting for what felt like way too long. Just the thought of hearing her voice made him quicken his steps until finally he was walking down the row of houses situated on the outskirts of town.

His feet landed nimbly upon the wooden planks, barely making a sound as he reached out to tap upon the door frame with the handle of his walking stick. Bending at the knees, he lowered himself so he could see through a part in the curtains and glimpsed inside.

Homes's heart came to a stop when he saw that Bonnie Shaughnessey was not alone in her living room. It wasn't a big surprise seeing Pamela Caudry there, but the other face was what had caused the breath to seize up in the back of his throat.

The man sitting in the living room next to Pamela fit every last bit of the description given to him by Tom and Kyle when they talked about Clint Adams. Not only was he sitting there looking at Bonnie the way Homes himself should have been doing at that instant, but he reached out and took her hand as though taunting him from the other side of the window.

It took every last bit of willpower Homes had to keep from smashing in the window with his cane and throwing himself at that smug bastard Adams. He could have also drawn the gun that hung at his side beneath his suit coat and that thought alone took twice as much energy to push back down into where it had come from.

After staring through the window long enough to imprint every last detail of what he'd seen into his mind, Homes straightened up and stepped away from the glass pane. His hand was frozen with walking stick in hand, ready to knock on the door.

Suddenly, Homes felt his entire body fill with an intense, angry heat. His knuckles turned white from gripping the walking stick so tightly and his hand itched to have the gun inside its grasp. The only thing that burned him more than his rage was the pressure of his firearm against his hip, which practically screamed at him to be drawn and used.

But that's probably exactly what Clint Adams wanted.

Nodding slowly to himself, Homes turned and stepped down off the porch. His feet made only slightly more sound than a cat as he dropped down to the street.

THIRTY-FIVE

When Clint walked back into the sitting room, he found Bonnie right where he'd left her, holding the letter in her hands. The only difference was that the letter was unfolded and she had even less color in her face than before.

Pamela went right over to the redhead and sat down beside her. She offered Bonnie her glass of lemonade, which the redhead immediately took and nearly drained.

"Thank you," Bonnie said. She seemed out of breath and once she let the cool lemonade past her lips, her hands began to shake. The letter rattled between her fingers, making it sound as though wind was passing over the pages of a book.

Not knowing exactly what to say, Clint stepped over to one of the chairs closest to the window and sat facing the distressed woman.

At that moment, Pamela asked the question that was on both her and Clint's minds. "Did you read the letter?"

Bonnie started to talk, but wound up only nodding before taking another sip of her drink.

"What did it say?"

Clint's first reaction was to try and get Pamela to stop asking so many questions. But once he saw that Bonnie seemed willing to speak, he held off on changing the subject. After all, he wanted to hear the answer as much as anyone else.

"It was personal," Bonnie answered. Looking over to Clint, she added, "Mostly just sentimental things to me about how he feels and how much he missed me. Nothing that might be of any use. I meant to thank you for bringing this to me, Mister . . ."

"Adams. Actually, you can call me Clint if you'd prefer."

"Right. Clint. Pamela mentioned your name, but my mind isn't all here lately. Thank you so much for bringing me this letter. It does my heart good to read it, but I'm not sure it was worth all your trouble."

Clint leaned forward and put his hand on top of Bonnie's. Looking into her eyes, he smiled and said, "Just having you feel better from reading it makes it worth the ride. I hope this helps you deal with your loss."

Returning his smile, Bonnie looked more alive than she had this entire time. In fact, the subtle change made the entire house feel a little more alive. "It does help, Mister Adams. It really and truly does."

Suddenly, Clint felt the hairs on the back of his neck stand up as though someone was watching him or creeping up from behind. He didn't want to alarm the women, so Clint eased himself back into his chair and calmly took a look around. The feeling had already passed by the time he turned to look casually out the window. Besides that, he swore he could see something move out on the porch for just a split second before it was gone.

"This is terrible," Pamela said as she jumped in to comfort her friend. "But you can make it through this. That's why I'm here."

Clint took the opportunity to get up and turn to face the window. Still taking his time, he pulled the curtains aside and gazed out to the street. There wasn't much to see out there. Just a few people strolling in small groups and one man who looked like a banker or some other type of businessman, who spent their days decked out in expensive suits.

When he turned around to look once again at the women sitting on the sofa, Clint found Pamela looking back at him. She had one arm around the redhead and was patting Bonnie's back while smiling up at Clint. By the looks of it, Bonnie was doing better. She still might have a few tears left to shed, but she didn't seem as distant as before.

"Oh, I almost forgot," Clint said while reaching into his pocket. "I have something else for you. It was something else Jack had that I meant to give you."

Clint reached for the pictures that were folded in his shirt pocket. When he removed the bundle, he quickly flipped through them until he came to the one marked ME AND BONNIE. Folding up the others and stuffing them back into his pocket, Clint handed the picture he'd selected over to the redhead.

She took it, smiled, and closed her eyes. The way she held onto the photograph, it seemed as though she was soaking up even more memories from the treated paper. "I don't know how I can thank you for all of this, Mister Adams. These things are the last things I have from Jack."

"Just so you know, his horse is at the livery and—"

"Yes," Bonnie interrupted. "I know about the horse. Ed told me all about it and just to be safe, you'd better not try to go near that horse. Ed gets awful protective sometimes."

Clint nodded and said, "Yeah. I noticed that myself. I was going to say I left the horse there for you since you're the closest one I could find to a rightful owner. If there's anything else I can do for you, just let me know."

"You've done so much already, but thanks for the offer. I'll be fine." Bonnie paused and looked down at the letter and photograph in her hands. "I'll be just fine now."

"That's good to hear. If you don't mind, I'll leave you two alone."

Pamela got up and asked, "Do you have to leave?"

"Actually, yes. I've got some business with the sheriff."

"Then let me walk you outside."

"That's not necessary, but if you insist." Clint put his hat back on and tipped it to Bonnie. "Nice to meet you. Maybe next time it'll be under better circumstances."

Bonnie smiled one more time. "I'd like that."

Stepping outside, Clint and Pamela shut the door and walked down the steps. Once they were in the street, Pamela turned and spoke to him in a voice that was just slightly louder than a whisper.

"Where are you going?" she asked.

"I'm taking the sheriff to Jack's body."

"I thought you might ask Bonnie about Luanne Parkinson. You were asking me about her plenty of times."

"First of all, I only brought her up once or twice. Second of all, take a look at this." With that, Clint removed the bundle of photos and flipped through until he found the one of the blonde and redhead together. "Does it look like Bonnie was too happy to be in this picture?"

Pamela only had to look at the image before she shook her head. "No. I guess not."

"Exactly. It seemed like she was barely holding herself together as it was back there, I figured I didn't need to bring up something else that I'm sure would be another sore subject." After refolding the pictures and putting them away, Clint said, "I'm not done looking into this. Maybe I won't even have to worry about this Luanne. I think I first need to have a talk with whoever sent that punk kid after me last night."

"You mean Andy Homes."

"I guess so. Right now, I need to get to the sheriff's

office before he has me hauled in by my boot straps. Will you be all right here by yourself?"

Pamela laughed once and propped her hands upon her hips. "I was fine before you got here, Clint. I can take care of myself after you go. Or should I say, I'll somehow find the strength to move on?"

"All right, all right. Don't be a smart ass. I'll check in on you in a few days. I might be gone for the better part of a week, since Jack's body is a pretty healthy ride from here."

"Well, hurry back. I'll make sure the Canyon Inn keeps that room available for when you get here."

"Well, if I know you'll be waiting in that big bed, I'll put the spurs on and make better time."

THIRTY-SIX

There were three reasons Andrew Homes kept one of his offices in town on the top floor of the Trailside Hotel. First of all, the owner owed Homes so much money that he let him keep the entire floor to himself for next to nothing. Second, the Trailside was nice enough that it gave him bragging rights to conduct business there. Finally, the hotel was right across the street from the sheriff's office.

Three of the rooms on that floor had gotten their walls knocked down and were combined into one big room. That was Homes's main office and all of the furniture was on the side of the room farthest from the windows. That way, he could sit behind his desk and look out at the city like a ruling emperor.

Unlike most other times when he was in his office, Homes now stood in front of the windows, looking over the curtains, which hung over three-quarters of the glass. He only had to lift his chin slightly to see over the curtain rod and down onto the front of Sheriff Gellar's office.

"So how good is this information of yours?" Homes asked without looking away from the window.

Behind him, Tom and a few of the others working for Homes shifted on their feet and glanced nervously at one another. Finally, Tom took the lead and spoke up.

"We heard one of the deputies talking when he had his coffee this morning. He said Sheriff Gellar expected to meet up with Clint Adams sometime before noon."

"Is that a fact? And what makes you think that he wasn't just spouting off to impress a waitress?"

Tom started to defend what he'd said, but stopped when he realized he didn't have much to back it up. He looked around to the trio of other men standing beside him, getting nothing but shrugs and sideways glances for a reply.

"He, uh . . . wouldn't lie to me, Mister Homes," Tom finally said. It was all he could come up with before the silence was dragged out any more.

"You'd better hope not, because I just saw Clint Adams at Bonnie Shaughnessey's house and it sure didn't look like he was in a hurry to leave. What about Miss Parkinson? Did you send someone to fetch her like I asked?"

"Yes, sir."

"Then all I need to see is her face and Clint Adams with the sheriff and you might just still have a job at the end of the day."

Homes kept looking through the window, shifting idly from one foot to another as the men behind him started to sweat. He could feel their tension like a wave of heat pressing on his shoulder blades. Finally, it got to be too much for Tom to bear and he stepped up.

"I know Miss Parkinson's on her way," Tom said. "And I'm pretty sure that the deputy was telling the truth. If he knew someone else was listening in on him, he might have—"

"You can quit your backpedaling," Homes interrupted. Nodding toward the window, he said, "Have a look."

Although he wasn't too comfortable with getting close enough to be within striking distance of that walking stick, Tom moved up to stand at Homes's side. He kept the well-dressed man in the corner of his field of vision and glanced out the window. As soon as he saw Clint Adams walking into the sheriff's office, he let out a deeply relieved sigh.

"I knew he would be there," Tom said.

As if on cue, there was a knocking at the door and someone walked into the renovated hotel room. Tom turned to look and felt even better when he saw the kid he'd sent out a few minutes ago standing there next to a blonde with one of the most impressive figures he'd ever seen.

But Tom knew better than to be caught staring too hard at the woman. That was an even quicker way to wind up eating a piece of Homes's walking stick. "And here's Luanne. Just like you asked."

That was the only thing that got Homes to look away from the window. He spun on his heels and brought the walking stick in front of him, tapping it down onto the floor as his eyes locked with the blonde's.

Luanne wore a cotton dress that hugged her figure as though it missed her when she wasn't wearing it. The bodice wasn't cut too low, but it didn't have to be cut too low for her to be testing the garment's seams. Her breasts swelled from within their restraints and seemed even more impressive by the fact that they were held up from underneath by a corset, which cinched her waist in tight enough to nearly fit within a man's hands.

Her hair was so blonde that it resembled polished gold. The only time it looked brighter was when it caught a stray bit of sunlight, which also showed off the smooth perfection of her skin. When she stepped into the room and spotted Homes, she smiled with full, pouting lips and hiked her skirt up enough so she could run to him.

Homes met her halfway across the room, smacking one of the boys in the back of the head for the offense of not knowing better than to stare at the boss's prize. Holding open his arms, he braced himself as Luanne bounced into his embrace and threw her hands around him.

"I heard you wanted to see me and I just had to run over here," she said in a high-pitched voice. "It feels like it's been forever since I saw you!"

"Yes it does," Homes said as he swept her off her feet and spun her around. "I've only now been able to finish up my business and get some free time to myself. What have you been doing, my dear?"

"Waiting to hear from you. Oh, and I fixed my nails."

Setting her down, Homes didn't so much as glance at the blonde's outstretched hands. "They look lovely. Absolutely lovely."

"So are you going to spend the day with me? I've been so lonely. It seems like nobody even talks to me when you're not around."

"That's because folks around here know I'll have whoever so much as looks at you killed the moment I find out about it."

Luanne and Homes both found that comment very amusing. None of the other men in the room, however, were even starting to crack a smile.

"It does feel like a long time since I've seen you," Homes said while taking Luanne's hand and leading her to another door. "Why don't we talk about it where we can be alone?"

"Are you done with all of your business, then?"

"Yes, my dear. Just about."

THIRTY-SEVEN

Holding open the other door leading from his office, Homes stepped aside and let Luanne walk in ahead of him. While most of the hotel's top floor had been turned into his office, the remaining three rooms had been combined into his own private suite.

The floor was covered with a carpet that cost more than most of the residents of Estes Canyon made in a year. It was soft and thick enough to mute any footsteps down to a barely audible rustle. Along one wall was a short bar that was fully stocked with Homes's favorite liquor. To keep up appearances, he had his favorite brands of whiskey poured into bottles bearing expensive labels. If anyone ever noticed, they certainly knew better than to point it out.

There were two chaise lounges. One sat on either side of the room, framing a large bed set within a polished brass frame. On top of the bed frame was a thin canopy, which hung down exotically. When he'd bought that piece of material, the man in the back of the wagon had told Homes that he'd gotten it from the streets of Paris. Naturally, that was the same story Homes fed back to anyone else who stepped into that room.

As soon as the door was closed, Homes strode across the room and glanced down at the street through the window. Although it was from a slightly different angle, he could still get a nice view of the sheriff's office from there.

Homes only had to wait a couple seconds before he saw Sheriff Gellar's door open and a group of men walk outside. Two of the faces were immediately recognizable. One was a deputy that Homes knew, but not too well. The last two through the door were Clint Adams and Sheriff Gellar himself.

Smiling, Homes stepped back from the window before one of those men down below happened to look up and see him. Now that he was sure Adams was in the hands of the law, Homes felt the weight upon his shoulders ease up a bit.

"Mmmm," Luanne purred as she stood next to the bed and let the material of the canopy flow between her fingers. "This French silk feels so good. I want a bed just like this."

"Then it's yours," Homes said as he walked toward the bed. "I'll have one just like it sent to your house and we can break it in together."

Luanne snapped her head around to look at him so quickly that strands of golden hair dropped down over her face. She smiled, blinked a few times, and swiped it away. "Show me how you want to do that," she said in a seductive whisper. "Show me right now."

Apparently, that was all the talking she planned on doing. Before Homes could walk close enough to touch her, Luanne had already unhooked the fasteners on the side of her dress, which kept the material wrapped so tightly around her torso. Sliding her arms out from the top of the dress, she wriggled back and forth, which allowed the garment to drop down to her waist.

No matter how many times he'd seen her, Homes was constantly taken aback by the sight of Luanne's naked body. Her large breasts swung slightly as she eased the dress down over her waist and then finally stepped out of it entirely. Large, dark brown nipples grew firm and erect as she moved her hands up along her sides until she could finally cup her breasts while letting out a subtle moan.

Homes reached out for her and placed his hands upon her hips. She responded with another moan as she tossed her head back and pinched her nipples between thumbs and forefingers. He looked down at the rest of her body, marveling at the way her hips swelled out to form a perfect hourglass shape. Even the trimmed hair between her legs was soft as down.

Allowing himself to indulge his every desire, Homes let his hand wander between her thighs, his fingers drifting through the wisps of blonde hair covering her vagina. She was already getting wet beneath his fingers, squirming ever so slightly as he allowed the tip of his index finger to slide between the lips of her pussy.

Luanne giggled softly while tugging open Homes's jacket and shirt. She undressed him with efficient expertise, peeling away the layers of his suit without snapping off a single button. Her freshly tended nails scratched along his bare skin just enough to send a chill through Homes's body. His jacket and shirt flew across the room to land on one of the chaise lounges.

THIRTY-EIGHT

Lowering herself to her knees, Luanne unfastened Homes's belt and opened his pants. She looked up at him while slowly taking down his pants. When they were all the way down around his ankles, she looked at the hard column of flesh that was standing erect in front of her full, parted lips.

Once she'd tossed the pants on top of the rest of his clothes, Luanne turned her face toward him and opened her mouth. She leaned forward and extended her tongue just enough so that it was the first part of her to touch his cock. Still moving forward, she opened her mouth wide and took him inside, sliding her tongue along the bottom of his shaft.

Now it was Homes who let out a soft moan as he stared down at her and moved his fingers through the locks of Luanne's hair. It felt as though he was moving his hand through strands of pure silk as he placed one hand at the back of her head and urged her to take even more of him into her mouth.

Once he was all the way inside, Homes felt Luanne close her lips around him and pull her head back as though she was savoring a lollipop. She even started to make a satisfied purring sound, which he could feel vibrating against his skin.

After licking him up and down slowly a few times, she closed her eyes and began sucking him faster. Luanne tightened her lips around him and bobbed her head back and forth, sucking loudly every time.

Homes felt his orgasm starting to build, but didn't want to finish just yet. Instead, he pulled away and held her head back when she tried to continue going down on him. He reached down and took hold of her shoulders, easing her to her feet and maneuvering her around so that she was standing against the bed and he was in front of her.

Luanne's skin was perfectly smooth and appeared almost golden in the room's light. Sliding his hands down along her body, Homes lowered himself to one knee and then gently teased the edges of her vagina with the sides of his thumbs.

When she felt him touch her there, Luanne dropped down onto the bed and lifted one foot up so that it was sitting on the edge of the mattress. She kept her other leg dangling down, spreading her knees apart as Homes pressed his mouth between her thighs.

Her pussy felt soft and hot against his lips. Homes didn't taste her because she liked it, but because it was what he wanted to do. She always told him after they made love what an attentive man he was, but the truth was that he did whatever the hell he wanted to her. If she got pleasure from what he did, then that was fine, but that wasn't his goal.

Tonight, Homes had a different goal. He did want to make her feel as good as possible and he knew that this was something she always responded to. He enjoyed the feel of her smooth sex on his mouth, that was for certain. He even liked the feel of her as she got wetter beneath his tongue and cried out when his fingers slipped inside of her every now and then.

When he thought about what was to come, however, Homes couldn't help but get even more excited. He ran his tongue up over the silky lips of her pussy one last time before standing up and taking a breath.

Luanne's eyes were wide with excitement and she all but jumped up of the bed as well. "Don't stop, baby," she begged. "Don't you dare stop."

Wrapping her arms around his neck, she pressed herself against him and rubbed one leg up along his shin. Homes could feel the firm warmth of her breasts pressed against his chest and when she ground her hips forward, he felt the dampness between her legs gliding over his cock.

Inside Homes's chest, his heart was pounding and the blood was rushing loudly through his ears. Acting on pure instinct, he took hold of her with one hand on her thigh and the other on her tight buttocks. From there, he clenched her to him and lifted her up just enough so that he could take her with him as he moved to the closest bedpost.

He didn't spare a moment for gentleness as he pushed her back until she all but slammed against the post, causing the entire bed to shake. Judging by the look in her eye and the sharp intake of breath that caused her chest to jump, Luanne didn't mind the rough treatment one bit. In fact, she held onto him that much tighter and even leaned in to playfully bite his shoulder.

"You like that, don't you?" Homes snarled under his breath.

"Yes."

"What about this?" As he said that, Homes shifted his hips until he could feel the tip of his cock pressing into her vagina. With just a little thrust, he was inside of her and Luanne's nails dug into his back and shoulders.

She flattened herself against the post and wrapped one leg around his waist.

"Do you like that?" Homes asked as he pumped in and out of her while looking directly into her eyes.

Knowing that there were other people in the next room, Luanne had been trying to keep her voice down. But once she felt the powerful thrusts of his stiff penis moving in and out of her, she couldn't hold back any longer. She started to say, "Yes," but the word became a passionate cry that filled the entire room.

Homes pushed all the way inside of her and stayed there, shifting a bit every now and then just to make Luanne squirm even more. He then took hold of her buttocks in both hands and lifted her up until she was able to wrap her other leg around his waist. Now she could lock her ankles behind him and held on tightly to his shoulders with both hands for support.

Being held up like that, Luanne felt as though she might fall at any moment. That nervous sensation in her stomach felt more exciting than anything else and only added to the erotic sensations that coursed through her entire body.

Now that he was in complete control of her, Homes pulled her back less than an inch just so he could reposition her lower body. When he pumped into her again, he drove inside even deeper than before, causing the bed to shake and Luanne to let out another moan of ecstasy. He found himself lost in the moment, clenching his eyes shut and thrusting into her harder and harder, faster and faster until Luanne's voice nearly echoed in the large room.

"Oh god," she screamed. "Yes! Yes!"

THIRTY-NINE

Homes could feel his own excitement building to its climax. The harder he fucked her, the more Luanne seemed to love it. The truth was that he'd never seen her so excited and that fact alone made his own orgasm that much more powerful.

After burying his cock inside of her one more time, Homes exploded within her. When he came, he let out a groan that sounded more like a growl than anything stemming from pleasure. Luanne smiled and tossed her head to one side, growling like him and laughing a little bit, too.

Once the last waves of pleasure had pulsed through him, Homes took a deep breath and focused his eyes on Luanne's face. She was still writhing and grinding against him, rubbing herself against the stiff shaft of his cock.

"You like that?" he asked. This time, however, he asked the question without a shred of emotion in his voice.

Luanne wasn't able to answer right away. She tried to talk, but could only get out a few gasping breaths as her own orgasm took hold of her and wouldn't let go. Finally, her body went limp and she relied on Homes to carry her over to the mattress.

He set her on top of the soft blankets and laid her down

with her legs hanging off the side. With his penis still hard and partly inside of her, he moved on top of Luanne and ground against her. She responded with a breathless moan while clawing at the sheets with both hands.

"You like that?"

"Yes," she finally replied. "God, yes I like that."

"Did you like it when he fucked you better?"

Still reeling from the intensity of her pleasure, Luanne let out another breath and opened her eyes. "What was that, baby?"

Homes's voice became steely and cold. "I asked if you liked it better when he did this to you. When Jack fucked you. Did you like it?"

Luanne's breath caught in the back of her throat and her body stiffened beneath him. Suddenly, she tensed as though she felt trapped under his weight rather than excited by having him on top of her. "I don't know what you—"

Homes cut her off with a swift backhand that caught her square on the jaw. "You know goddamn well what I'm talking about! Answer the question, you whore!"

"Baby, this isn't funny anym—"

Homes reared up like an animal glowering down at its evening meal. He seemed even more savage to her since he was still naked and glistening with sweat. Pulling his hand back behind his head, Homes bared his teeth and snarled as he lashed out at her again.

The blow caught her on the cheek and was hard enough to roll her onto her side. "You fucked him! I know you fucked him! At least admit it, goddammit!"

Luanne dug her heels into the mattress and pushed herself back from him, covering her face with both hands. "I'm sorry. I didn't think you'd find out. I'm so sorry."

For a moment, Homes fell completely silent. "You didn't think I'd find out? Well that explains it, then. That makes it all right. What a good fucking person you are."

Once she'd put some distance between herself and Homes, Luanne lowered her hands and looked at him with a fire building up behind her own eyes. "It's not like we were married. You'd never ask me to marry you anyway, so why shouldn't I do whatever I damn well please?"

"You could have fucked this whole town for all I care. But you knew how I felt about Jack MacFarlane and you still let him put his dick inside you anyways. You filthy little slu—"

Moving faster than he would have imagined, Luanne darted forward and swung at Homes with her right hand. She wasn't exactly aiming or trying to do a lot of damage, but was more lashing out with nothing but pure anger behind her blow. Her right hand smacked against his chest and so did her left, which swung out hot on the heels of her first strike. She caught him with her nails on the second hit, leaving a set of shallow scratches in his flesh.

For a moment, Homes was stunned. He touched the spot where she'd hit him and felt the little bit of blood she'd drawn. He started shaking his head as though he couldn't believe it and moved back so he could get off the bed and onto his feet.

"You stupid whore," he said. "The only reason he had anything to do with you is because he knew how much I'd hate it. Whatever he told you, that was the only reason."

Her eyes flashed and she lifted her chin defiantly. "Oh yeah? Well he said that exact thing and I took him to my bed anyway. He was a good-looking man, and he could at least keep it going for more than a minute or two."

With that, the entire room became deathly still.

Nothing moved.

Not Homes.

Not Luanne.

Not even the air.

Finally, pulling in a slow, controlled breath, Homes

walked around to the side of the bed where he could get closer to Luanne. She stayed where she was, glaring at him as if daring him to say something else.

But Homes didn't do anything. Instead, he simply stood there and looked down at her.

Luanne swore she could feel his stare piercing a hole through her body and drilling out the other side. She was too angry to let him know that he was scaring her, however. So she kept her composure until he finally turned away.

Letting out the breath she'd been holding, Luanne raced to think of what she should do next. She wanted to get out of that room, but knew the other room was filled with men in Homes's employ. The only thing that came to mind was that she had to get out of there. If she had to run naked through a crowded room to do so, then that would be better than spending another moment inside that bedroom.

Homes moved like a cat through the dimly lit room. Walking over to his pile of clothes, he bent down and reached for the crumpled pieces of his suit. Rather than take his pants or shirt, he dug through until his hand closed around what he was truly after. He stood up, hefted the walking stick in his hand, and turned his attention back to Luanne.

FORTY

At first, the men sitting around in Homes's office were amused by the sounds that came from the adjoining bedroom. They'd all savored every glimpse they could get of Luanne Parkinson, but knew better than to get caught with their eyes on the busty blonde. When her passionate screams could be heard through the walls, all of the cowboys had quieted down to listen.

They resumed their conversations when the room next door had gone quiet, but started listening again when the other screams began. First came the recognizable sound of Homes's angry rants. Then came Luanne's frightened reply followed by more swearing from Homes.

Tom jumped to his feet when he heard the sound of someone being struck. The reaction was instinctive and nearly brought him crashing through the door. When he saw that none of the others were going to back his play, Tom stepped back and tried to ignore the sounds that followed.

There was no more screaming, but there was plenty of dull thumping sounds that could only be fists against flesh. Soon, all of the cowboys lowered their eyes when they could tell that it was no longer a fist being pummeled against bare skin.

Each one of those men had been on the receiving end

of that walking stick and knew the sound of it the way a mule knows the sound of a whip being cracked over its head. Those gut-wrenching noises didn't last long and soon heavy footsteps thumped around the bedroom. Not too long after that, the door flew open and Homes charged out.

Hastily tucking his shirt beneath his belt with one hand, Homes carried his walking stick like a bat in the other. Everyone in that office noticed the blood dripping from its silver handle.

"Give her a few minutes to get dressed," Homes said to the cowboys as a whole. "If she doesn't come out after that, I want her dragged out and thrown into the street."

Tom was closest to Homes and had to step back before the other man literally walked over him. "Maybe I should get the doct—"

"Two minutes," Homes barked. "Then toss her ass into the street." With that, Homes went to a small shelf near his desk that had a few glasses and a crystal liquor bottle on it. He plucked out the bottle's stopper and dropped it to the floor before filling the closest glass.

By the time he was bringing the glass to his lips, Homes saw Luanne peeking out from the bedroom. "You've got about a minute left, whore. Best use it before it's gone."

Luanne stepped out from the bedroom. Her dress had obviously been thrown on and she held it up to cover her since she hadn't taken the time to fasten all the clasps. Carrying her shoes in one hand, she moved out of the room and darted to the door leading to the hall.

The entire left side of her face was swollen and red. There was a trickle of blood coming from the left corner of her mouth as well as her nose. Judging by the way she walked, every step was painful to take. All of her muscles were tensed and yet she still couldn't get herself to move any faster.

Homes kept his eyes on her the entire time. After taking a sip of his drink, he put it down and smacked his walking stick against the side of his desk while lunging forward. He didn't charge toward her, but only stomped his foot down in front of him. That was more than enough to cause Luanne to jump and run from the room.

Grinning, Homes picked his glass back up and leaned the walking stick against the desk. "Now that I've taken care of that little bit of business, someone tell me about the other outstanding matter."

One of the cowboys who had been posted next to the window spoke up. He was an oafish-looking sort with a thick torso and ridged forehead. "If you mean Clint Adams, he took off with the posse and rode out of town."

"Excellent. Was that the same group I saw walking out of the sheriff's office a little while ago?"

"Yes sir, Mister Homes."

"Then that's another bit of business taken care of." Downing the rest of his drink, Homes stepped forward and held open his arms as though he was about to embrace all the men working for him. His smile was wild and victorious. "In fact, I want you to gather up all the others and tell them to meet me at the Full House Saloon so I can buy you all a drink!"

The cowboys nodded to one another and started heading for the door.

"What's the matter with you boys?" Homes asked. "Cheer up. This storm's just about behind us. In a day or two, I should be getting some news that will be good for everyone. For tonight, though, I feel like celebrating!"

FORTY-ONE

It was an easy matter of meeting up with Sheriff Gellar and rounding up some men to form a posse. In fact, it was so easy that Clint was just waiting for something to go wrong before they headed out of town. Then again, he knew the lawman wanted to keep an eye on him as well as collect Jack MacFarlane's body to verify another part of Clint's story.

Once Clint had made his presence known to the lawman, he and the posse were already storming back out the door. There was a quick stop at the livery so they could collect their horses and in a matter of minutes, all five of them were thundering out of town like they were charging off to war.

That enthusiasm lasted the first couple miles and was maintained as a way to let the horses stretch their legs. Once Estes Canyon was behind them and the open trail stretched out ahead, the riders fell into a comfortable pace.

Clint and Sheriff Gellar rode at the front of the pack. One of the deputies that Clint didn't recognize rode on the other side of him while Johnny and the third deputy rode at the rear of the formation. Clint was too busy enjoying the ride at first to think about much else besides that and making sure he was leading the party in the right

160

direction. As the day wore on, however, he got a distinct feeling from the lawmen around him.

Waiting until the horses had slowed down a bit and everyone had fallen into a mix of calm boredom, Clint looked over to Sheriff Gellar. "I'm surprised you didn't bring more men."

"Huh?" Gellar said, snapping himself out of his trance. "What was that?"

"You almost brought enough to keep me circled in here, but there's still an open bit of space right in front of me."

"First of all, I've got more than enough men to take you down if it comes to that. Just because you're the great and mighty Clint Adams doesn't mean you can dodge all of us.

"And second, if I was so concerned with keeping you fenced in, I would've left you in that cell back in town. Don't forget that I've got more than enough to hold you in jail for beating on Kyle. And after the things Ed told me, I'd be within my rights to hang you."

Although the sheriff's words were harsh, Clint could tell that he only meant some of them. "The only reason I brought this up was because I'm getting the distinct impression that you still don't trust me."

"Why? Because you've got two deputies riding at your back?"

"That, along with a deputy to one side and the sheriff on the other." Clint was used to riding with the law, but there was something coming from those particular lawmen that was making him uncomfortable. So far, none of the others had drawn their guns or even looked at him any particular way. There was still a hostility that Clint could feel around them and he wanted to know where it was coming from.

"We've got a ways to go if we're to follow the directions you were telling me about," Gellar said. "And me

and my men are going to be there every step along that
way, so you'd best get used to it."

"And what happens after we get there?"

"Then I take a look at this body to see if it really is
Jack."

"Then what?" Clint asked. "We bring him home and
then what? Do I go back into that cell so some liveryman
with a chip on his shoulder can testify that I'm a murderer
just because he doesn't like me? If I'm looking at jail
time or a trial, I'd like to know, Sheriff. I think I have
that right."

Gellar looked over at him and studied Clint for a few
moments. Finally, he turned in his saddle and glanced
back to the deputies following him. "You two ease up a
bit."

"But Sheriff, you said to—"

"Well, now I'm saying you can ease up. Give Mister
Adams some breathing room." Settling back into his saddle, he looked to Clint and said, "You've got good instincts, Adams. Tell you something else, you were right
to be suspicious. I had my doubts about you, but I've got
good instincts, too."

"And what do your instincts tell you about me?"

"That maybe I should give you the benefit of the
doubt." Gellar paused and smirked. "Or at least enough
rope so you can hang yourself. It would save me the has-
sle of doing it."

The lawman was able to keep a straight face for another second or two before it cracked into an even wider
smile. Clint joined him for a laugh along with the rest of
the men. Looking around at the deputies, Clint did notice
that they'd eased off a bit and were following at a more
normal distance. Besides that, Clint no longer felt the tension directed at him that had been there before.

It wasn't his place to say how the sheriff should conduct his business, but now that he wasn't under quite as

much scrutiny, he felt like he simply had more room to breathe. It made the rest of the day pass by much easier and by the time the sun began to dip below the horizon, Clint was actually even enjoying the ride.

They made camp just before the sun's light was completely gone from the sky. Between the five of them, they were able to find a clearing and gather enough wood to last throughout the night. One of the deputies got a fire going and the rest gnawed on some rations and beef jerky from their saddlebags.

Clint was in charge of brewing the coffee. Not only did he do that, but he also pitched in some beans as well to be cooked over the open flames. That, at least, put him in the good graces of the rest of the posse. The entire group ate their meals and drank their coffee, all without saying more than two words to each other the entire time.

Some of the tension was back and most of it was unmistakably directed at Clint. He could feel it, but knew that all of the lawmen were simply keeping their guard up around a known gunfighter and dangerous man. He didn't like to think of himself as either of those things, but Clint could see why others would.

He stretched out on his bedroll and slid his hat down over his eyes, knowing that he shouldn't lose any sleep over the suspicions of the men he was riding with. After all, they were just doing their jobs.

FORTY-TWO

The next morning was spent much like the previous night. The same deputy got the fire up and roaring again while Clint brewed the coffee. The only difference was that Sheriff Gellar chipped in by frying up a few slices of bacon for each man to have with their rations.

"You ready for another long day's ride, Adams?" Gellar asked.

Clint looked at him over the dented edge of his tin coffee cup. "Sure enough. It'll clear my head a bit."

"Well, nothing clears a man's head like a good ride. Except for a hearty breakfast."

"If it's all the same to you," Clint said while holding up a piece of burnt bacon, "I'd much rather have my breakfasts at the Canyon Inn."

Gellar's chest shook for a second as though he was about to cough something up. What came out of him was a boisterous laugh that startled the last remnants of sleep out of every deputy's eyes. "You can say that again," the sheriff boomed. "You sure as hell got me there."

Clint shared a little of the lawman's good spirits, but the simple fact of the matter was it was just too damn early to laugh that hard over anything. He enjoyed the fresh air as much as anyone but, bedroll or not, sleeping on the ground was sleeping on the ground. It would be another hour or two before Clint could enjoy the day as much as Gellar.

Before too long, the fire was kicked out, supplies were packed, and the posse was headed back on their way.

Hours slipped away along with the miles and for a while, Clint could sit back in the saddle and simply enjoy the feeling of speeding over the earth. Eclipse's breath churned from his nostrils like steam from a train's engine and his powerful legs thudded against the ground in a constant flow of motion.

The land was beautiful, wrapped up in autumnal colors and before Clint realized it, the sheriff was calling them all to a stop to give the horses a rest. Pointing off the trail, the lawman steered them to a watering hole that only he and the youngest deputy, Johnny, knew about.

"That's one hell of an animal you got there, Adams," Gellar said.

"He sure is."

Stepping up a little closer and lowering his voice to just above a whisper, the sheriff added, "You could outrun every last one of us on that thing, couldn't you?"

Clint held the lawman's stare and nodded once. "Probably. But keep one thing in mind, Sheriff."

"What's that?"

"I didn't."

Gellar didn't say anything else, but he was clearly letting that thought soak in. The rest of the day's ride was quiet and uneventful since most of the deputies started keeping each other company rather than keep their eyes on Clint every moment they could.

Sheriff Gellar made occasional conversation with Clint, but nothing much more than he would to some stranger standing next to him at a bar. For his part, Clint was glad that he didn't have to worry about thinking of things to say. He didn't mind one bit just easing back, relaxing, and bantering with Gellar whenever those few opportunities presented themselves.

One thing that became obvious as they rode was that Clint had been going even faster than he'd thought when he'd ridden from the grave into Estes Canyon. By the rate the posse was riding, they might have to tack on at least an extra twelve hours before they got to their destination.

After working that out in his head, Clint tried to spur the entire group along by pulling in front of them just enough to get them to follow. He knew he'd only draw more suspicion onto himself if he raced ahead, so he sped up just enough so that they might just pick up their pace reflexively. It was a delicate balance to maintain, but it also gave Clint something to occupy himself throughout the day.

Surprisingly enough, after the sun had made its own path across the sky and the group was settling into their campsite for the night, Clint actually felt more relaxed than when he'd started. For a change, he didn't have to dodge any bullets or think about some punk strutting up to him and starting a fight.

The simple life definitely had its advantages. Letting out an easy breath, Clint didn't feel much weight on his shoulders at the end of that day. Well, not any additional weight, anyway. There was still the business that had brought them all out on this ride to begin with that needed wrapping up. And there was plenty more to deal with back in town. For the moment, however, Clint only had to build a fire and have some dinner. It didn't get much simpler than that.

Judging by the quietness of the entire group, the lawmen were in the same frame of mind as Clint. Either that, or they were too busy worrying about their own duties to bother with making conversation. Clint didn't really care which it was.

Quiet was quiet.

FORTY-THREE

They ate their rations and drank their coffee. The breeze was already colder now than it had been the night before, causing all of the men to lift their hands to the fire and gather their coats and jackets a little tighter around them.

"Winter'll be here before you know it," Gellar said.

The rest of the men nodded and sipped their coffee.

"Well, one thing's always good on a cold night out in the middle of nowhere."

"Yeah," Johnny said. "Whiskey."

Gellar reached into the inner pocket of his coat. "Well, the next best thing then." Taking his hand out, he produced a bunch of cigars and started passing them out to each man. He paused in front of Clint, but then handed one over to him as well. "Go on, Adams. It'll warm you up a bit."

Not wanting to be rude, Clint took the cigar and nodded his thanks. Although he enjoyed the occasional smoke, he wasn't much of a connoisseur of the things. It was simple reflex, however, for him to lift the cigar to his nose and sample its scent.

He recognized the smell immediately. However, the last time he'd smelled it, the scent had been mixed in with the faint hint of brass.

"What's the matter, Adams?" Gellar asked. "You don't

like the cigar? I apologize if it's not the best, but it's my normal brand. You'll just have to rough it like the rest of us."

Pretending not to notice the sarcasm dripping from the lawman's tongue, Clint bit down on the end of the cigar and ripped it off. "Not at all, Sheriff," he said after spitting out the nub. "I could use a light, though."

Gellar reached out and grabbed one of the smaller branches burning in the campfire. Taking his time, he chewed off the end of his cigar and spat it out while the branch crackled and smoked in his hand. He touched the bit of flame to his own cigar first before handing the branch over to Clint.

Using the flame to light his own cigar moments before it died out, Clint pulled in a bit of smoke while glancing around the fire. He studied each deputy in turn while rolling the cigar between his fingers as if savoring the tobacco.

The youngest deputy didn't interest him. In fact, Johnny was the only one of the lawmen who didn't seem interested in the cigar he was offered. He held it without lighting the end, much like a boy pretending to act like the men around him.

The other two deputies sat on the other side of the fire, opposite both Clint and Sheriff Gellar. Those two had been the ones watching Clint the closest throughout the ride and it was to them that Clint looked next.

One of them had already lit his cigar and was puffing away. The second was leaning back with his shoulders resting against a large rock. His legs were stretched out and crossed as if he was lounging in a hotel suite of his own.

Watching that one from the corner of his eye, Clint took special interest when he saw the deputy reach under his jacket and pull out one end of a small chain. He used the end of the chain to poke a hole into the end of the cigar, twisting the metal piece around and digging it in farther until he was satisfied with the job. Only then did he put the cigar in his mouth and reattach the chain to something beneath his jacket.

"So tell me," Clint said, turning to face the youngest of the deputies. "Did any of you men know Jack Mac-Farlane?"

"I spoke to him some," Johnny answered. "He was a nice enough fella."

Although Clint nodded casually and smoked his cigar, he was listening intently to every word that was spoken. Not only that, but he was studying the men as they spoke, searching for anything that struck him as unusual. It was a skill picked up from the card tables that had become almost as valuable as his skill with a gun.

Sometimes, more so.

"Jack was a good man." It was Sheriff Gellar who gave that testimonial. Clint watched him as well, but didn't have to study as hard since he'd already taken so many mental notes on the lawman.

Exhaling a pungent, smoky breath, Gellar leveled his eyes on Clint. "Why else would I go through so much trouble to find him?"

Clint shrugged and shook his head. "Just making conversation." Once the tension had eased up a bit, he turned to the other two deputies. "What about you two? I feel like I've been going through an awful lot for this Mac-Farlane and it'd sure be nice to know something about him."

The deputy farthest away from Clint shrugged and attempted to blow a smoke ring into the air. He failed. "I didn't know him. He had some trouble with Mister Homes, though. Everyone knows that."

"Yeah," the third deputy said as he stretched out a bit more. "He and Andy never did see eye to eye."

Clint glanced over to that man, but in fact turned all

of his focus onto every little thing the deputy was doing.
"I heard they fought. What was all that about?"

"I don't know how it started."

Clint knew even before the man was done talking that
he was spouting out a lie. There was a distinctive twitch
in the corner of his mouth along with a smugness in his
eyes as though the deputy thought he was pulling something over on someone.

"And how did he die?" Clint asked.

All of the lawmen were a little surprised by the di-
rectness of Clint's question, but the deputy lounging
against the rock seemed momentarily stunned.

"He . . . must've been shot by robbers or such," the
man stammered.

Once again, Clint's gut told him that was a lie.

Frustrated, the deputy said, "Hell, I don't know. We'll
find that out when we get the body, I guess."

Clint nodded and puffed his cigar. In the back of his
mind, he was certain they were about to find out a whole
lot of things.

FORTY-FOUR

It was a good thing that Clint had found the last couple days so restful because he didn't get more than a few winks of sleep that night. His mind was too busy mulling over the things he'd learned around the campfire and his senses were too busy looking out for him throughout the darkest hours of the night.

By the time the sun crested over the horizon, Clint was ready to get some things out in the open. He knew he couldn't do any of that just yet, however. There was a time and a place for everything and it was important that he waited for the right time and place to make his next move. Besides that, there was more he could learn in the hours separating them from their goal.

Of course, there was also the trick of making it to the end of the ride without getting himself killed.

Thanks mostly to Clint and Eclipse speeding up the entire pack, the posse made it to Jack MacFarlane's resting place at just before dusk that day. Knowing that he would at least be telling someone how to get there, Clint had made special efforts to remember where it was. After passing the first landmark that was near the grave, Clint had signaled for everyone to slow down so he could concentrate.

It was only a matter of following his mental notes before Clint was headed straight for a pile of freshly turned earth marked by a cross formed from two sticks lashed together. They all dismounted and stood in front of the grave.

"You did a real nice job, Adams," Gellar said. "It's almost a shame that we have to dig it up."

Johnny let out a haggard breath. "Jesus, do we really have to do that, Sheriff?"

"Just shut up and start digging. That goes for all of you. I need to make sure that's really Jack under there. For all we know, this could be just a mound of dirt."

Grudgingly, all of the men started digging with small shovels that had been packed onto the back of Johnny's horse. It didn't take long before one of them hit something more solid than just dirt.

"I think I found it," one of the deputies said.

Sheriff Gellar moved over to where that man was standing and pushed him aside. Bending at the knees, he moved aside the dirt until he came to what had stopped the other man's shovel. Clint was looking down from the other side of the hole and immediately recognized the jacket he'd used to wrap up the body.

All of the men either stepped back or turned away when they were hit by the stench of death that flowed up from the ground. The reeking odor hit them all like a brick, causing Johnny to stagger away to somewhere he could puke up his breakfast.

Finally, Gellar pulled the leather aside and looked down at the dirty, contorted face. "Yep. That's Jack, all right." Looking over to Johnny, the lawman said, "You can head back and let the others know we found him. Make sure Jack's relatives get the news as well."

"Mister MacFarlane had family in town?" Johnny asked.

"Find that out. Just go on and get out of here. That's an order."

Although not too happy with being forced to leave, the youngest of the lawmen seemed relieved once he was away from the rest. He got on his horse, paused, and looked over at Gellar.

"I said get going," the sheriff barked.

That was all Johnny needed to get him speeding on his way.

Clint watched the kid ride off and then turned to face the sheriff. "It's a bit late for him to be taking off, don't you think?"

"No. Just help me pull this body out of here."

The grisly job took less than an hour to complete. Most of that time was spent digging out the rest of the corpse and lugging it up out of the hole. From there, the two remaining deputies draped the body over one of their horses and tied it down.

"We can make camp here," Sheriff Gellar said. "And we'll head back in the morning."

Clint went over to the body and acted as though he was making sure the bindings were tight. Suddenly, he pulled back and looked at the ground. "What was that?" he said. "Did anyone else see something shiny drop out of a pocket or something?"

The first man to look down was the deputy who'd been savoring his cigar against the rock the night before. "What're you talking about?"

"Right there," Clint said, pointing down.

The deputy stepped over and squatted down. Once the deputy was rooting around in the mess of dirt and fallen leaves, Clint reached into his own pocket and stepped back.

"Looking for this?" Clint said as he allowed the watch he'd found in Jack's pocket to drop down and dangle from its chain.

Sheriff Gellar walked forward and stared at the watch hanging from Clint's fist. "Where did you find that?"

"Recognize this, Sheriff?"

"Sure I do. It's Blake's watch." Turning to face the deputy that had been searching on the ground, he asked, "When did you lose your watch, Blake?"

Clint found it mildly amusing that he'd pieced together so much about that deputy without even knowing the man's name until just now.

Standing up, Blake shrugged and said, "That ain't my watch. I was just looking here because he said he saw something drop. I got my watch right here." With that, the deputy removed his watch and held it in the palm of his hand. Apart from the cover being slightly less dented, the two timepieces looked identical.

"Open it up," Gellar ordered.

Blake pushed down the watch's pin and snapped the cover open. The innards were also the same, right down to the pearl face and black roman numerals. It even started playing a familiar tune.

Snapping open the watch he'd found, Clint showed it to the sheriff as the music was echoed between both watches.

"So what?" Gellar asked. "Blake's got his own watch. What are you trying to prove?"

Clint threaded the watch chain through his hand until he got all the way down to the fob. Lifting it to his nose, he took a sniff and held it out toward the sheriff. "We all saw Blake here preparing his cigar last night. I'm sure that's not a new habit. It just seems spooky to me that the owner of this watch mysteriously has the same habit."

After sniffing the end of the chain, Gellar shifted his eyes toward Blake. "And that even smells like my cigars. What the hell is this, Blake? What's going on here?"

"Yeah, Blake," Clint said while snapping the watch shut and handing it to Sheriff Gellar. "What's going on here?"

Blake backed away, glancing around nervously at the

other deputy who remained at his side. "He's the one we should be looking at here," he said, jabbing a finger toward Clint. "He's the one who knew right where the body was."

Clint squared his shoulders at the fidgeting deputy. "He said something, didn't he? Jack said something or was going to say something that made you cut him up like a piece of meat."

"If anyone cut that asshole's tongue out, it was you, Adams!" Blake shouted. "I'll bet you killed him and are just trying to cover your ass."

"I think you're the guilty one here," Clint said. "Especially since I never told anyone about Jack's tongue being cut out."

FORTY-FIVE

None of the men said a word. For a moment, they all just stood rooted to their spots. Finally, Sheriff Gellar walked over to the body, opened its mouth, and took a look inside.

"That's no shit, Blake," Gellar said. "His tongue's not in there." Facing Clint, the sheriff dropped his hand down and drew his gun from its holster. "And yours won't be where it's supposed to be either. Not when we get done with you."

Clint felt the bottom drop out of his stomach and cursed himself for not being even more suspicious of everyone in the group.

The sheriff kept his gun pointed at Clint as the two deputies drew theirs as well. "And don't bother trying to impress us with your quick draw, Adams. That Colt hasn't been loaded since yesterday and neither of us has let you out of our sight long enough to reload."

"I already figured as much. After all, you wouldn't let me have a loaded gun after going through all the trouble of getting me out here so you could bury me. So what did Jack find out? Was it that your deputy was working for Mister Homes? Or did he learn more than that?"

"No. That was enough to get the tongue ripped from his skull. Jack had a lot of friends, so the message had to be nice and bloody so they'd remember what happens to folks who talk too much."

Blake stepped forward and glared at Clint. "How the hell did you know about me and Mister Homes?"

"The watch. I guessed it was yours only last night. It's a pretty fancy piece of craftsmanship and looks more than a little expensive. The only man I've heard about in Estes Canyon that could afford not only one, but two of those things is Andrew Homes. It only fit since he was the one who had the feud with Jack all along. But you know what really cinched it?"

"What?"

Smirking, Clint said, "You just told me."

"You smart-mouthed son of a bitch," Blake spat as he stepped up and swung his pistol around to knock Clint in the face.

Moving in a blur of motion, Clint reached out to take hold of Blake's gun hand and twist it around so the pistol was turned sideways in his grasp. He kept his momentum going, which pulled Blake off his balance as he was dragged around in front of Clint's body.

Clint slipped a finger over Blake's trigger finger and pressed down hard. The deputy's gun barked once as Clint stopped turning. The bullet from Blake's gun roared out of the barrel and slammed into the chest of the other deputy. The second deputy staggered back a step and was blown completely off his feet when Clint forced Blake to squeeze his trigger another time.

Another gunshot roared through the air and Blake grunted once in agony as a slug tore into his back.

Clint grinned as he wrenched the pistol from Blake's hand and let the deputy go. He'd kept hold of Blake's arm so the other man's body would be between himself and the sheriff, but he hadn't thought that Gellar would truly take a shot at him through his own man. Apparently, that was the second time he'd been wrong about the lawman. He was determined there wasn't going to be a third.

"Hold it right there," Gellar said as Blake dropped to the ground.

Clint's hand was caught in midaim and was pointed halfway between the sheriff and where the second deputy had been standing. He did as he was told, keeping his body still and his arm where it was.

"Drop that pistol and take out your Colt."

Clint let the gun drop from his hand, stepped around so he could face the sheriff, and removed the Colt from its holster. "Why go through all this? With Jack, I mean. Wouldn't it have been easier to just kill him somewhere nobody would find him like you're doing with me?"

"Yeah, it sure would have been easier," Gellar said. "But you try telling that to a rich asshole who doesn't do anything unless it's a show."

"Homes?"

"Who else? He's the richest man in town and he doesn't care who knows it. He only cares if there's someone that doesn't know. And I sure knew the day it was that Jack MacFarlane made the mistake of bedding down with that golden-haired blonde Homes is so fond of. Not only that, but Jack even had pictures taken of himself and both his own woman and that blonde that belonged to Andrew, just to rub salt in the wounds."

"That blonde would be Luanne Parkinson," Clint said, picturing the second woman in the photograph.

"It sure would. I guess ol' Jack ran out of ways to get under Homes's skin. He didn't have the power, money, or muscle to do any damage to the rich man, so Jack hit him below the belt.

"Homes asked me to kill Jack the same night he found out about MacFarlane and Luanne. It was supposed to be a spectacle so I tied Jack up to his horse and was about to put a bullet into him when he started trying to talk his way out of it. He said he'd seen me and Homes talking and that he knew I was taking the rich man's money. He even said some of his friends would tell all they knew about it if anything happened to him."

"So you cut his tongue out? Not too subtle."

"There's not a damn thing about this feud that's subtle, Adams. The whole thing's a circus and I was just playing along."

"What if Jack was bluffing?" Clint asked. "Why couldn't you just scare him out of town and let him live?"

"I couldn't take that chance. You should know that."

"Yeah. I guess I was just checking to see if you had a soul left."

Sighting down his barrel, Gellar said, "I sold that a while ago, Adams. But you don't need to worry about that. Whenever someone finds you, they'll see those bodies laying there, you laying here, and that gun in your hand. Of course, it'll be loaded by then, minus a few rounds to make it look right. But that'll be the end of this whole damn mess and to hell with all of it."

"So this is all over a woman," Clint said. "Why not just ride away now, Gellar, before you pay an even higher price for another man's vanity?"

"Too late, Adams. I'm in too deep."

Clint waited until he could see the sheriff's finger tightening around his trigger. Only when he was absolutely certain the lawman going to fire did he whip his hand forward and throw the Colt into Gellar's hand.

The Colt bounded off the lawman's fingers, forcing Gellar's first shot to go high and wide. Clint was already dropping to the ground and rolling forward. A shot echoed through the air as he passed over the gun he'd thrown— his gun—and a bullet drilled into the earth an inch away from Clint's skull. With his gun in hand, he stuck out one leg to stop his movement.

Clint wound up laying on his side. He lifted his hand and squeezed off a round without taking more than a frac-

tion of a second to aim. Instead, he merely locked his
eyes on where he wanted the bullet to go and let his reflexes do the rest.

His gun barked one last time, spitting a piece of lead
through the air that drilled a hole through Sheriff Gellar's
forehead.

Clint was back on his feet before Gellar's body finally
toppled over and crashed into Jack MacFarlane's open
grave. Stepping over the other man's twitching leg, Clint
looked down and said to the body, "I never carry an un-
loaded gun!"

Just then, a horse thundered toward the gravesite and
Johnny swung down to take in the scene. "What the hell
happened?" the deputy asked. "I heard shots."

Clint looked over at the kid. "You had to know these
men weren't right. You may be young, but you don't
strike me as stupid. You had to know what they were
doing."

Johnny's head lolled forward as though he couldn't
bear to look Clint in the eyes. "They always tried to keep
me from seeing what they were doing. That is . . . after
Mister Homes tried to give me money the first time."

"Then go back to town and spread the word."

"What about the rest of them? What about Mister
Homes?"

"I'll go with you, then. Once the truth comes out, I
don't think they'll try to do anything to you anyway. Especially since the rich man doesn't have his ace in the
hole anymore."

"I . . . I tried to warn someone," Johnny stuttered.
"Well, I tried to warn whoever might find the body. When
I saw they meant to run him out of town on his own horse,
I tried to give out a warning."

Suddenly looking at the kid with new understanding,
Clint asked, "Were you the one who took Blake's watch
and put it in Jack's pocket?"

Johnny nodded. "He was always bragging about that watch. He told me it was one of a kind and that there wasn't no other like it. He nearly lost his head when it came up missing. I was hoping the horse would come back and someone would find it."

"Well, it may have taken the long way of getting there, but the horse came back."

Johnny nodded and looked at the bodies laying on the ground. He looked especially hard at the sheriff staring up from the hole in the dirt. Clint looked down at them as well. The faces of the dead stared back at him, just as he was sure they would stare at him for a long time to come.

"Come on, kid," Clint said as he led Johnny away. "Let's get back to town. I can't wait to see the look on that rich man's face when he finds out the wrong two people made it out of this."

FORTY-SIX

Andrew Homes had been drinking and celebrating for three days straight. Thinking that he was not only rid of Jack MacFarlane but had even arranged to dispose of the legendary Clint Adams, he figured he had a hell of a lot of reasons to raise his glass. Now that Luanne was no longer in the picture, he'd been sampling every lady in town who had a taste for his money. So far, he was in no danger of seeing the same one twice in a row.

"What have we here?" he asked while peeling off his clothes and making his way to the shape that lounged on top of his bed in the dark.

The silhouette was impressive. Rounded in all the right places, the woman's skin shone in the light like it had been bathed in cream. In fact, Homes hadn't seen a body as perfect as this one since . . .

Homes froze with his hands still in the middle of lowering his pants to the floor. "Luanne?" he asked.

The blonde crawled forward on top of the bed. When her face was more in the light, the dark bruises and large welts became more visible. Even still bearing the evidence of the beating he'd given her, Luanne managed to smile.

The next thing to catch the light was a small revolver in her hand. "Your boys are letting anyone with tits into this room nowadays. You should be more careful."

"I . . . I'm glad you're back."

She nodded, pulled back the hammer of her pistol, and fired a round into Homes's chest. Since he didn't drop right away, she sent another round into his already quieted heart.

Getting up, she looked down and spat on his twitching face. "Did you like that?" she asked.

Just then, the door to the bedroom burst open and Kyle raced through.

Luanne tossed the gun down and crossed her arms in front of her. "What are you going to do now? Kill me?"

Kyle shrugged. "I might have, but you shot the man who would've paid me to do it."

"Then I'll pay you and the rest of the boys to forget about it. Andy's safe was hid behind the—"

"No need for that, darlin'," Kyle interrupted. "We all know right where it is."

Watch for

THE ONLY LAW

261st novel in the exciting GUNSMITH series
from Jove

Coming in September!

JAKE LOGAN
TODAY'S HOTTEST ACTION WESTERN!

Explore the exciting Old West with one of the men who made it wild!